Praise for

WHEN THE WOMEN
COME OUT TO DANCE

"Let the last line of dialogue from Elmore Leonard's new short-fiction collection sum up Mr. Leonard's great gift: 'He could tell a story.' More precisely, he can invent coolheaded characters who leap off the page, equip them with pricelessly terse dialogue and dream up the kinds of plots that might have worked for O. Henry, if O. Henry had had a serious interest in lowlife, double-crossing, and crime. The short-story format brings out these strengths to a surprising degree."

—Janet Maslin, *New York Times*

"Leonard's prose is a delivery system honed to bring fans quick hits of pleasure. The effect of this, his thirty-ninth book, is to leave you a little high and definitely addicted to the author all over again."

—New York *Daily News*

"Other writers have to downshift to write a short story. Leonard's not-one-word-wasted style doesn't have to be changed a lick. His craftsmanship is such that many readers won't even notice it—which is the highest compliment one can pay."

—*Philadelphia Inquirer*

"Elmore Leonard's . . . most accomplished female characters in years."

—*USA Today*

"Vintage Leonard. . . . With *Dance* we get nine stories with booze and shotguns and lowlifes in them and lots of scenes that ought to be in movies. . . . What recommends this book to Leonard fans most is that many of the characters are beloved ones from earlier novels."

—*Detroit Free Press*

"This collection of short fiction by the top crime writer proves Leonard knows all the moves to keep readers in step with him. Enlivened with wisecracks and wry observations, Leonard's prose will have readers shaking with chuckles, rattling with tension and rolling right along with the beat of his fabulous plotting."

—*Boston Herald*

"The title story is as fine a piece of writing as Leonard has ever done."

—*Oregonian*

"The voice is there, dry and with a hint of what lordly amusement would sound like if God had worked at a Detroit ad agency. . . . In the shorter form, [Leonard is] masterly."

—*San Jose Mercury News*

LINDA SOLOMON

ELMORE LEONARD has written more than
three dozen books during his highly successful
writing career, including the bestsellers *Tishomingo
Blues, Be Cool, Get Shorty,* and *Rum Punch,* and his
newest novel, *Mr. Paradise.* Many of his books
have been made into movies, including *Get Shorty*
and *Out of Sight.* He is the recipient of the Grand
Master Award of the Mystery Writers of America.
He and his wife, Christine, live in a suburb of
Detroit.

www.elmoreleonard.com

ALSO BY

ELMORE LEONARD

An Imprint of HarperCollins*Publishers*

ELMORE LEONARD

WHEN THE WOMEN COME OUT TO DANCE

stories

For my friend Otto

The following stories were originally published in other works: "Sparks" in *Murder and Obsession,* edited by Otto Penzler, in 1999 by Delacorte Press; "Hanging Out at the Buena Vista" in *USA Weekend,* June 13, 1999; "Chickasaw Charlie Hoke" in *Murderers' Row: Baseball Mysteries,* edited by Otto Penzler, in 2001 by New Millennium Press; "Fire in the Hole" as an e-book in 2001 by Contentville Press; "Karen Makes Out" in *Murder for Love,* edited by Otto Penzler, in 1996 by Delacorte Press; "Hurrah for Capt. Early" in *New Trails: Twenty-three Original Stories from Western Writers of America,* edited by John Jakes and Martin H. Greenberg, introduction by John Jakes, in 1994 by Doubleday; "The Tonto Woman" in *Roundup: An Anthology of Great Stories by the Western Writers of America,* edited by Stephen Overholser, in 1982 by Doubleday.

A hardcover edition of this book was published in 2003 by William Morrow, an imprint of HarperCollins Publishers.

HarperCollins books may be purchased for educational, business, or sales promotional use. For information please write: Special Markets Department, HarperCollins Publishers Inc., 10 East 53rd Street, New York, NY 10022.

First Dark Alley edition published 2004.

DESIGNED BY SHUBHANI SARKAR

The Library of Congress has catalogued the hardcover edition as follows:

Leonard, Elmore, 1925–
    When the women come out to dance/Elmore Leonard.—1st ed.
      p. cm.
    ISBN 0-06-008397-2
    1. Detective and mystery stories, American. I. Title.
    PS3562.E55 W47 2003
    813'.54—dc21   2002026426

ISBN 0-06-058616-8 (pbk.)

04 05 06 07 08 BVG/RRD 10 9 8 7 6 5 4 3 2 1

CONTENTS

SPARKS

They sat close to each other on the sofa, Canavan aware of Mrs. Harris' scent and her dark hair, parted to one side, she would hold away from her face to look at the map spread open on the coffee table.

Canavan was showing her the areas destroyed by fire, explaining how the hot Santa Ana wind swept the flames through these canyons and on down toward the Pacific Coast Highway. Close to four thousand acres destroyed but only nine homes this time, including Mrs. Harris' Mediterranean villa, here, at the top of Arroyo Verde. Nothing like five years ago when over two hundred homes were lost. He showed her photographs, too, fires raging against the night sky.

Robin Harris said, "Yeah . . . ?" looking at the photos but not showing any real interest.

Canavan kept glancing at her, Robin a slim turn-on in a trendy kind of way: pale skin and heavy eyeliner, silver rings, designer-ripped jeans, barefoot, a black sleeveless top that showed the chain, tattooed blue steel, around her upper left arm, the one close to Canavan.

The profile he had in his case file described her as the former Robin Marino: sang with a rock band that played L.A. clubs, produced one album, gave it up five years ago to marry Sid Harris: the legendary Sid Harris, lawyer to platinum-selling recording artists. Now a widow at thirty-seven, Robin was estimated to be worth around ten million. She had lost Sid to a coronary thrombosis, at home, only three months ago, Sid sixty-three when he died. And had lost the house in the Malibu hills three weeks ago, close to a million dollars' worth of furniture and contents destroyed. But she had bought the Wilshire apartment, where she was living now, right after Sid's death. Why? It was on Canavan's checklist, one of the things he'd ask her about.

She said, "What's the point?" Meaning the map and the pictures. "I saw the fire, Joe. I was there."

Arriving, he had introduced himself and handed Robin his business card that said *Joseph Canavan Associates, Insurance Investigations.* She had looked at it and said, "Are you a Joe or a Joseph?" He told her either, but usually Joe. She said, "Well, come in and sit down, Joe, anywhere you like," picking up on his name in a way that sounded natural and gave him a glimpse of her personality. She looked at his business card again and said, "You're not with the insurance company, like the ones before." He told her they called him in when they red-flagged a claim, had questions about it. All it meant, certain conditions existed the company felt should be investigated. Canavan said they wanted to know in their hearts the fire was either accidental or providential before paying the claim. Robin said, "Well, I can tell you the same thing I told the fire department, sheriff's deputies, the state fire marshal's office, the California Forestry Department and a guy from Alcohol, Tobacco and Firearms. The fire marshal's guy brought a dog that sniffed around. He said when the dog was working it ate seventy Kibbles a day. What would you like to know?"

This was when Canavan first arrived.

Now he turned from the map to look at Robin sitting back in the sofa. She resembled a girl in the movies he liked a lot, Linda . . . very sexy, had an Italian name. He said, "I wanted to show you the path of the main fire, where it came down west of your place, on the other side of the ridge."

"So how did my house catch fire," Robin said. "Is that the question? How about sparks, Joe? The wind blows sparks over the ridge from the brush fires in Boca Chica and they land by my house. You buy that? Or a rabbit or a coyote caught fire and ran like hell right through my yard. They said on the news, look out for animals that catch fire and spread it around. Otherwise, I have no idea. Joe, I watched my house go up in flames. I might've stayed till it burned down, I don't know, maybe not. A deputy came up the road and made me leave."

Linda Fiorentino.

That was who Robin looked like, in that movie—he couldn't remember the name of it—where she goes in a bar called Ray's, remembering that because of the sign, the Y in RAY'S shaped like a martini glass. Linda goes in and asks for a Manhattan. The bartender ignores her and she asks him who you have to blow to get a drink around here. Those weren't the exact words, but that was the idea. Robin had that same effortless way about her, confident, with the New York sound like Linda's, a cool chick, tough. Watch your step with her.

"So you weren't living in the house at the time."

"I was here. I happen to see it on TV—fire trucks, people loading their cars, coming out of the house with their insurance policies, running around looking for pets. One guy had all their good china in a basket and was lowering it into the swimming pool. I thought, I better get up there, quick."

"Load your car," Canavan said, "with anything of value, uh? But I understand the house was already on fire. I think that's in the statement you made."

"By the time I got there, yeah." Linda waved her hand in the air. "The back of the house, by a brush thicket. Sid was supposed to have it cut back, but never got around to it. The sky by that time was thick with smoke."

"See, what the company wonders about, why your house was the only one on Arroyo that caught fire."

"I guess 'cause there aren't any close by. I'm at the very top of the road. Have you been up there?"

"I had a look at your place," Canavan said, "the chimney and some of the walls. What's hard to tell is where the fire started."

"I told you, in the brush thicket."

"Maybe, except it looks like the direction of the fire in the thicket was away from the house. I'm told the wind shifted that afternoon and came off the ocean."

"I don't know," Robin said. "It's always windy up there."

Canavan gathered the map from the coffee table. "You bought this place a few months ago?"

An easy question, but she paused before telling him, "Not

SPARKS 5

long after Sid died. But I haven't bought it. I'm leasing it furnished, nine grand a month with an option to buy."

Canavan looked around the formal living room, white and cream, touches of color, landscapes framed in gold tint, a garden terrace through the French doors, poppies and ficus trees fifteen stories above Wilshire Boulevard. A nine-thousand-a-month penthouse she might or might not buy. He said, "This place is worth as much as your house?"

"They'd go for about the same price," Robin said. "Two and a half million. Sidney said the house was underinsured. That's why, just before he died, he had the value of the policy increased."

"And when that happened," Canavan said, "and the house burns down soon after, the claim gets a red flag."

Looking right at him Robin said, "Well, you know Sid didn't do it. And I'd have nothing to gain, would I? I'd already made up my mind to sell the house."

"That's why you moved out?"

"It's too lonely up there. Just me and the coyotes. Once they ate my cats, both of them, Puddin and Mr. Piper, I bought a shotgun, see if I could even the score, a twenty-gauge Remington. But then a couple of deputies came by to tell me I had to stop shooting. A neighbor had complained. Some woman said I was shooting toward her house. I go, 'What neighbor? I don't have any neighbors. She might've heard shots, but how does she know I'm the one shooting?' They said she saw me."

"Mrs. Montaigne," Canavan said. "She uses binoculars."

It caused Robin to pause and he felt her looking at him with new interest.

"How do you know that?"

"I spoke to her. Mrs. Montaigne's a self-appointed fire warden. Twice a day she drives to a spot up on Piuma Road, near Rambla Pacifico, and looks for smoke. She lost a house in '93 and had it rebuilt."

"She actually saw me shooting coyotes? I'm a good mile below Piuma Road."

"Not as the crow flies. I went to see her, talk to her about spotting fires, and she surprised me. Said she saw you the day your house burned down."

"Saw me where?"

"At the house. She spotted the main fire and called the county fire camp. They were already on it. Still, eight houses burned to the ground."

"Nine," Robin said.

"She saw your car, too, the Mercedes convertible?"

"Yeah, as soon as it came on the news I got dressed, jumped in the car . . ."

"But why the convertible?"

"Why not?"

"If you were going there to save some more of your stuff, and it might be your only chance . . . Don't you have a Range Rover?"

"I was thinking about the *house*," Robin said. "I wanted to find out if it was still there. I'd already picked up my jewelry, moved out most of my clothes."

"There wasn't anything else of value?"

"You have a list, don't you, on the claim?"

"In my file. I haven't really looked at it."

"It's all Asian art, Chinese, some authentic, some copies.

But even if I'd brought the Rover there wouldn't have been room for the big pieces."

"So for about three months the house was locked up, nobody there?"

"I'd spend a weekend."

"Alone?"

She smiled, just a little. "Where're you going with that, Joe?" And said, "No, I wasn't always alone."

He smiled the same way she did, just barely. He said, "You got up there and the house is on fire."

"Yeah, but I didn't see the flames right away. I told you, the fire started on the other side of the house, away from the road."

"You say in that thicket."

"Yeah. You have a problem with that?"

"I might," Canavan said. "According to Mrs. Montaigne, you were there a good twenty minutes to a half hour before there was smoke or any sign of a fire. And she had a pretty good view of the back side of the property."

There was a silence.

"In fact, she said she saw you go in the house."

Robin took her time getting up from the sofa. She said, "Joseph," walking across the room to a bar with a rose-tinted mirror behind it, "what would you like to drink?"

"Whatever you're having," Canavan said.

Straight-up martinis. He sipped his watching Robin roll a perfect joint, tips of her fingers working but not looking at it, Robin asking in her Linda Fiorentino voice why

he would want to be an insurance company stooge, Jesus, or
why anyone would—Canavan letting it happen, giving Robin
time to make her play. She said, "No, first let me guess where
you're from. The Midwest, right?" He saw this could take
time, so he told her he was from Detroit, born and raised.
Came out to sunny California six years ago. She wanted to
know what he did in Detroit and Canavan said:

"I was a police officer."

She said, "Jesus, really? What kind?"

Radio cars and then ten years on the bomb squad. Offered a
job out here with an insurance company, investigating claims,
before setting up his own company. He said he'd learned to
recognize arson from working on the bomb squad. See what
Robin thought of that.

She was cool. Handing him the joint she said, "You left out
your wife."

"I don't have one," Canavan said, hoping this was a variety
of weed that inspired wit and not the kind put you to sleep.
He took a pretty good hit and passed the joint back to Robin.

She said, "You don't have to tell me if you don't want to,
but I'll bet anything you had a wife at one time."

He told her yeah, he got married while he was a cop. They
came out here, he happened to get involved with a girl at the
insurance company and his wife found out about it.

"She divorced you for *that*?"

"You'd have to know her," Canavan said.

"So it wasn't the first time."

He told her it was, as a matter of fact, the first and only
time he ever fooled around.

She didn't believe him. Lying back among little pastel

pillows on the white sofa Robin raised her eyebrows. She said, "Really? You look to me, Joe, like the kind of guy, if it's there you don't pass it up. You still see her?"

"Who?"

"The girlfriend."

"That was over before it went anywhere. I see my ex-wife now and then, we go out to dinner. Sometimes she does jobs for me. Chris's a photographer." He picked up the raging-fire shots from the coffee table. "She took these. Chris takes long-lens shots of people walking around who claim they can't walk. A guy shooting hoops in the backyard who's supposed to be in a wheelchair. Insurance fraud situations, all kinds, including arson," Canavan said, bringing it back to Robin.

No reaction. Ducked that one like she didn't even hear it, saying, "You go to bed with her?"

"What's between Chris and me," Canavan said, "stays between us. Okay?"

"That means you do," Robin said. "You keep Chris for backup, right? Call her when you haven't scored in a while." Robin pushed up from the sofa with her empty glass. You ready? One more—I have to go out tonight."

Her husband dies and three months later fire destroys the house. Canavan wondered if there was a connection. He had no reason to believe there was; still, he didn't rule it out. He watched Robin sipping her martini. The only apparent effect the gin had on her, she spoke in a quieter voice and stared at him. Canavan could feel a buzz; combined with the weed it allowed him to stare back at Robin, time suspended, and ask her whatever he felt like asking.

"When you got married, did you have to sign a prenuptial agreement?"

She said, "Don't worry about it."

So he tried another tack. "How'd you and Sid meet?"

"He saw me perform and we talked after. He asked me out. He knew who I was. But basically, Joe, we got together the way people usually do, and fell in love."

"He was a lot older than you."

"What you're asking now, did I marry him for his money. Sure, that had a lot to do with it, but I liked him. Sid was full of energy, played tennis—he'd sit down and cross his legs you'd see his foot going a mile a minute. You want to know how he was in bed? Not bad, though we had to get almost perpendicular—you know what I mean?—to do it."

"Wasn't he kind of heavy?"

"That's what I'm talking about. But then toward the end he lost a lot of weight, like thirty pounds. No, Sid was tender, very gentle, till Viagra came along and he turned into Attila the fucking Hun. If you can picture that."

"I thought he had a heart condition."

"It wasn't serious. He took something for it. His blood pressure was a little high."

"And his doctor let him have Viagra?"

"Sid got it over the Internet."

"But he must've known the combination was dangerous, Viagra and heart medication?"

She said, "Joe, Sid was a shooter. He didn't get where he was being cautious. It helped he was a genius."

"You were happily married."

"Yeah, very."

"But you fooled around a little."

"Once in a while I'd find myself in a situation. You know, but it was never serious. Like you and the chick from the insurance company." She sipped her drink and then finished it. "I'll tell you the truth, Joe, I miss him. Sid was good to me." She got up with her empty glass saying, "You're ready, aren't you?"

"I thought you were going out."

"I changed my mind."

Watching her cross to the bar he said, "Tell me something," and watched her looking in the mirror, staring at her image, her pale skin tan in the tinted glass.

"What do you want to know?"

"Why you burned your house down."

Robin didn't answer until she was coming back with the martinis, her raccoon eyes in the dark liner holding on Canavan.

"Why would I?"

"That's what I'd like to know."

She gave him his drink and placed a hand on his shoulder as she edged past the coffee table and sat down again.

"You tell me," Canavan said, "you'd have nothing to gain, you were gonna sell the house. Now you don't have it to sell, but you get two and a half million when they pay the claim, plus the value of the contents."

"I could've sold the house for more, easy." Robin sipped her drink and said, "But what if . . . This is hypothetical, okay? What if a person does actually burn down her house? She owns the property, she can rebuild if she wants. She might even tell the insurance company to forget the claim."

"They'd want to know why."

"Because they piss her off acting so suspicious, dragging their feet, sending out adjusters and investigators instead of paying the claim. She's above dealing with people with small minds."

This was one Canavan hadn't heard before. He said, "Tell me how she starts the fire."

"She rolls up the *Wall Street Journal* and lights it with a match. The point I'm making, Joe . . ."

"She starts the fire inside the house or outside?"

"Inside. The point I'm making, they can pay the claim or not. If they choose to, fine. If they don't, who's out anything?"

"She's already out the Mediterranean villa."

"And doesn't care."

"What makes it Mediterranean, looking down at the Pacific Ocean?"

"Tile roof, big oval windows and doors. The outside wasn't bad, even though pink's not one of her favorite colors. It's the inside of the house she can't stand. The decor throughout, the furniture, the art, floor to ceiling everything's Chinese. And she doesn't even like Chinese food. Listen, I can roll us another one if you want."

"Not for me."

"It's local, Malibu Gold, but pretty good, huh?"

Canavan said, "Yeah, great," and asked Robin, "Why didn't this hypothetical woman change the decor?"

"Her husband loved it. He knew what everything was and where it came from. It was like a culture thing with him. He becomes an expert on something besides picking hits. Incidentally, not one of the artists he represented ever made a record that stiffed."

"He bought all the Chinese stuff?"

"His previous wife, the second one. They redecorated completely after a trip to China."

Canavan said, "You couldn't . . ." caught himself and said, "She couldn't get used to it?"

"Joe, it was like living in a fucking pagoda. Jade figurines, Tang horses and tomb figures, that honey-colored huanghali furniture, blue-and-white Ming garnitures, they're vases, Ming kesi panels on the walls, ink paintings, opium beds, snuff bottles, ivory carvings, coromandel screens, Quing dynasty court rugs . . ."

"She could've sold it."

"Cloisonné enamel incense burners, Sung dynasty Buddhas. Five years," Robin said, "she lives with all this Chinese shit cluttering up the house. Big, heavy pieces, the tomb figures almost lifesize. Five years, Joe. She begs her husband, 'Please, can't we try something else?' No. 'A Mediterranean house, why don't we do it Mediterranean?' No. Not 'No, and I don't want to hear any more about it.' Her husband was a cool guy for his age, never raised his voice. But, really, it was all she thought about. She'd smoke a jay and scheme. Like hire a burglar; he takes it out a piece at a time. Or have it done all at once while they're in Cabo, or Maui."

"Once her husband's gone," Canavan said, "why didn't she get an auction house in and sell it?"

"She felt it would be disloyal to his memory and it would be on her conscience."

Canavan thought that was interesting. "But it's okay if something happens to it."

"Yeah, like an act of God."

"Or a fire, in an area known for its fires. You know who you remind me of?"

"Linda Fiorentino."

"You look just like her."

"I know."

"That movie where she goes in the bar . . . ?"

"*The Last Seduction*. She wants a Manhattan and the bartender won't look at her. So she goes, 'Who does a girl have to suck around here to get a drink?' "

That was it. Not who do you have to blow.

"But as I was saying, when you come right down to it, Joe, who's out? Who's hurt? Who gives a shit outside of this person who owns the house?"

"I'll tell you who," Canavan said, "if you really want to know. The law. Arson's a second-degree felony. A conviction can get you two to twenty years. There's a death as a result, it goes up to five to ninety-nine."

Her reaction: "For Christ sake, Joe, come on. You want to put me in *jail*?"

"I'm not the law. All I'm supposed to do is let 'em know when I see a crime's been committed."

She said, "Joe, come on, you're not a snitch. I can tell you're a very practical guy. How much you want?"

Like that, ready to pay him off.

He said, "What's your best offer? So we don't waste time."

"How about fifty grand?"

"You can do better'n that."

"A hundred?"

He said, "Mrs. Harris," and paused. "You mind if I call you Robin?"

Sounding formal now, and he could see she didn't know what to expect, hesitating before she said, "Sure, why not," in a kind of vague tone of voice, her mind looking ahead.

He said, "Robin, you've talked to a lot of people. Fire, law enforcement, insurance company stooges . . . One of 'em even brought a dog out to sniff around. But no one's accused you of burning your house down, have they?"

She shook her head and brushed that soft, dark hair away from her face.

"You drive up to the house, the sky's full of smoke. You've already seen houses burning on the TV news, and they're right over in the next canyon, not half a mile away. You're thinking, Damn it, why can't my house catch on fire?"

She was nodding, staring at him with a thoughtful expression, following every word.

"You go inside and stand there surrounded by all this oriental stuff you hate."

"You don't say oriental, you say Asian."

"Either way, you hate it. You stand there looking at all that lacquered stuff, Buddhas and dragons, and you light a joint."

He watched her raise her eyebrows.

"The joint is to take the edge off, calm you down. But now you look at the match in your hand. It goes out and you light another match and look at the flame."

She was nodding again, staying with him.

"All that smoke, and remembering what you saw on the news, you're convinced sooner or later your house will catch fire."

"I was, I was sure of it."

"You're about to lose part of your life, and there's nothing you can do but stand back and watch. Five years up in smoke."

Robin waited.

"What you do then is part acceptance and part a farewell gesture to the years you spent here with Sid."

"Yeah . . . ?"

"You light the *Wall Street Journal*."

He watched her nodding her head, thoughtful now. She looked up at him and said, "You're not putting that in your report, are you?"

Canavan shook his head. "I have no evidence to prove it, or disprove what you said. The house was burning when you got here."

"What about the lady fire warden?"

"Mrs. Montaigne? She must've been mistaken."

Robin paused and said, "How do I pay you the hundred thousand?"

"You don't," Canavan said, getting up from the sofa. "I was playing with you, that's all. Seeing what I could score if I did that sort of thing. You should hear some of the offers I get, I come across a fraud situation and I can prove it. Some bozo in a neck brace looking for a million bucks, says he'll split it with me."

"You turn them in?"

"If they're pros, like the ones that stage car accidents and people are injured. Or if they get ugly about it. Otherwise I tell 'em, forget the claim and don't try it again."

"You're not turning me in?"

"I told you, I believe your story."

"So what should I do?"

"If I were you?" Canavan said. "I'd keep after the insurance company. Make 'em pay." He turned to leave, saying, "It was nice talking to you, Robin."

And saw her raccoon eyes staring at him.

"You can't stay a while, Joe?"

If he didn't stay, he could always come back.

HANGING OUT AT
THE BUENA VISTA

They lived in a retirement village of cottages set among palm trees and bougainvillea, maids driving golf carts. The woman, Natalie, wore silk scarves to cover what was left of her hair, a lavender scarf the afternoon Vincent appeared at her door. He told her through the screen he thought it was time they met. She said from the chair she sat in most of the day, "It's open," closed the book she was reading, a finger inside holding the page, and watched him come in in his khaki shorts and T-shirt.

"You didn't have to get dressed up on my account."

She liked his smile and the way he said, "I was right. I've found someone I can talk to."

"About what?"

"Anything you want, except golf."

"You're in luck. I don't play golf."

"I know you don't. I checked."

She liked his weathered look, his cap of white hair, uncombed. "You're here by yourself?"

"On my own, the first time in fifty-seven years."

She laid the book on the table next to her. "So now you're what, dating?"

He liked the way she said it, with a straight face.

"If you're interested, Jerry Vale's coming next week."

"I can hardly wait."

He said, "I like the way you wear your scarves. You've got style, kiddo."

"For an old broad? You should see me in a blond wig."

"A woman can get away with a good one. But you see a rug on a guy, every hair in place? You can always tell."

"That's why you don't comb your hair?"

Again with the straight face. He shook his head.

"I made a decision," Vincent said. "No chemo, no surgery. Why bother? I'm eighty years old. You hang around too long, you end up with Alzheimer's, like Howard. You know Howard? He puts on a suit and tie every day and calls on the ladies. Has no idea where he is."

"Howard's been here. But now I think he and Pauline are going steady. Pauline's the one with all the Barbie dolls." Natalie paused and said, "I'll be eighty-two next month."

"You sure don't look it."

"Not a day over, what, seventy-five?"

"I'll tell you something," Vincent said. "You're the best-looking woman here, and that's counting the maids and the ones that pass for nurses. Some are okay, but they all have big butts. You notice that? Hospitals, the same thing. I've made a study: The majority of women who work in health care are seriously overweight."

"You've spent a lot of time in hospitals?"

"Now and then. No, this is the closest I've come, this assisted living. Or as it says in the literature, 'The gracious and dignified living you deserve.' As long as you can afford it, live in your own prefab cottage. I did all right with prefab, built terraces, row housing. Some, it turned out, in the wrong place. Andrew came along and blew 'em off the lot." He said, "I know you were married. What'd your husband do?"

"Commercial real estate."

"I might've known him."

"In New York City."

There was a lull. Vincent glanced around the room, at furnishings from another life, expensive-looking pieces.

"You're happy here?"

"Am I happy?"

"I mean, do you like living here?"

"It's all right."

He waited before saying, "Are you in pain?"

"I have my pills."

Vincent nodded. "Back 'em up with a cocktail in the evening, against orders."

She said, "Do you always wait till evening?"

"Hardly ever."

Natalie stirred, pulling herself up. "You can have whatever you like as long as it's Polish vodka."

"You want me to get it?"

She said, "Sit still," up and moving now: slim brown legs in a white shirtdress that barely reached her knees. He could see her fifty years ago, taller, not as frail, dark hair in place of the lavender scarf, a confident, good-looking woman. She returned with drinks in crystal glasses, handed him one and settled back into her chair with a groan. Now she was looking at him again.

"Don't you have drinking buddies?"

"The guys here," Vincent said, "the ones who know where they are, either play golf and talk about it on and on, or they sit and watch CNN all day. I get the feeling they miss Ronald Reagan."

She sipped her drink. "Is it a matter of time with you?"

"I'm given maybe six months. What about you?"

"Anywhere from a few months to 'who knows?' "

"Are you afraid?"

"Not so much anymore."

He said, "You learn to live with it."

And she smiled. "In a manner of speaking."

"'Maintaining a quality of life,'" Vincent said, quoting the literature again, "'to which you're accustomed.' Only this isn't what I'm accustomed to. Hanging out, not doing anything."

"Waiting," Natalie said. "No, I'm not either." They sipped their drinks in silence, not a sound coming from anywhere in the house or outside, in that green glare of vegetation in sunlight.

"You want to get out of here?" Vincent said.

It surprised her. "What do you mean?"

"Take off? Go somewhere?"

Natalie said, "I suppose we could," nodding her head.

"Or," she said after a moment, "you could get your pills and move in here with me. What do you think?"

Now Vincent was nodding in the same thoughtful way.

"Would we sleep together?"

Natalie took a moment before saying, "Well, not the first night."

CHICKASAW CHARLIE HOKE

This time Vernice started in on Charlie while he was making their toddies, what he did every evening Vernice worked days. Charlie said, "Take a load off your tootsies, honey, and let me wait on you."

She eased into her La-Z-Boy to sit there as she always did, leaving a space between her round thighs. Vernice was in her forties, younger than Charlie by ten years, a big redhead with the whitest skin Charlie had ever seen on a bare-naked woman. She started in by saying Carlyle, her brother-in-law, hired a family to work his soybeans and now had a job at the Isle of Capri dealing blackjack. It was always someone she knew, the manager of some podunk motel now a pit boss at Bally's. She'd mention the casinos were always looking for help or desperate for it.

Charlie would say to her, "Honey, I'm not just help." This time he said, "Honey, can you see me dealing cards?"

"Carlyle says between tips and wages he can make up to a thousand a week."

"Those people do that kind of work are ro-bots," Charlie said, pouring bourbon over crushed ice, adding sugar now, an orange slice and a maraschino cherry. "Be a waste of what I'm good at."

"What, talking to people?"

"Talking, referring to my career, sure."

"You could tend bar."

Charlie smiled over at her, Vernice in her pink waitress outfit she wore at the Isle of Capri coffee shop. He said to her, "Can you see me in a little red jacket and bow tie? A grown man my size grinning for tips?" Charlie was six-four and would put his weight at around, oh, two-forty if asked. He had a gut that wasn't too noticeable on his frame. He had a nose he said was his Chickasaw Indian heritage and eyes like a hawk; he'd set the palm of his hand above his eyes and squint to demonstrate. Seeing himself in one of those little red jackets caused Charlie to shake his head.

He said, "I don't work for tips—" without thinking, and wanted to grab the words out of the air. Shit. Like a ball you throw to curve low and away and the son of a bitch hangs letter-high on the batter. He stepped over to Vernice with her drink. "I know what you're thinking, that I don't work, period, but you're too nice a person to hurt my feelings."

"What you do," Vernice said, "is talk."

"Yes, I do."

"Tell baseball stories over'n over."

"Honey, baseball's my life."

"Oh? And what's it pay now, fifteen years later?"

This didn't sound like his honey speaking. It was now sixteen years since he'd played ball, but he didn't correct her.

Now she said, "Tell me what I'm getting out of this arrangement?"

He wasn't certain what she meant, but said the first thing in his mind. "You get *me,* you get my companionship—"

"I get to hear you talk," Vernice said, "is what I get. I get to fix you supper, I get to loan you money . . ."

She paused to think of something else and Charlie said, "Till I'm back on my feet. I didn't quit that bingo hall 'cause I don't like to work. I told you, how'm I gonna talk to a bunch of old women don't even know who I am? I need the right spot's all. Come on, you know me by now. How long we been together?"

He thought she might say too long, though it'd only been a couple months. No, this time she went right to the point saying, "I made up my mind. I'd like you out of the house, Charlie, by the end of the week. I can't afford your companionship any longer'n that."

He thought of a remark he could make if this was one of their usual arguments—Vernice fussing at him for not taking the trash to the dump and his saying, "Oh, I'm sorry, I didn't notice you broke your leg." He could say something about her calling this RV in a trailer park on the outskirts of Tunica, Mississippi, the South's Casino Capital, a "house." He could say, "Oh, that's what you call this tin box waiting on the next tornado?" But this wasn't an argument where you could say what you wanted and then take the trash to the dump.

She was giving him a deadline at the worst time, broke and needing a place to live; so he had to be nice. This wasn't hard because he did like Vernice, her usually quiet way, her pure-white body, her housekeeping. He told her one time cleanliness was a rule with the Chickasaws: a woman who didn't keep her house clean was marked, had her arms and legs scratched with dried snake teeth. It was true. He'd give her Indian lore and she'd roll her eyes. Or she'd say he was no more Indian than she was and Charlie would say, "Then how come they called me Chief all the years I played ball?"

Vernice brought him back to right now saying, "By week's end, Charlie. I'm sorry."

He turned to the counter and took time to screw the cap onto the Early Times bottle. He turned back to her saying, "What if I'm offered a position by then?"

"I love your choice of words, a position."

"As a celebrity host. What some of us do when we retire."

"Shake hands with the slot players?"

"Take care of the high rollers, honey, see they're comped to whatever they want."

"Like girls? You gonna be a pimp, Charlie?"

He let it go by. "Or I could set up the entertainment, special kinds of events."

"Well, let's see," Vernice said, "Andy Williams is at Harrah's, George Jones at Bally's. One of the Righteous Brothers is opening at Isle of Capri, taking over from that Elvis impersonator." She said, "If all ten casinos can get any big-name entertainers they want . . . ? You see my point?"

She must've seen it as a stopper, a question she could ask without even a smarty tone to her voice. Charlie said, "I got an idea I haven't told you about." Her or anyone at all while he watched the new hotel going up, from bare iron to stone, with a big goddamn tepee made of concrete rising a good three stories above the entrance. He said, "You know there's a new one opening next week. They got the sign up now, Tishomingo Lodge and Casino, Tunica, Mississippi."

It gave Vernice pause. "You been over there?"

"I'm seeing the fella runs it, Billy Darwin from Atlantic City, young guy. He was running Spade's and the people here waved enough money at him he moved to Tunica. I've seen him around—little guy, has hair like Robert Redford."

Vernice said, "Tishomingo, that's Indian."

"Chickasaw. Tishomingo was the big chief the time they got shipped off to Oklahoma. Follow me now," Charlie said. "Where was I raised? In Corinth. And where's Corinth? Clear across the state but only fifteen miles from the Tishomingo County line, where the Chickasaws came from originally. Some never went to Oklahoma and're still around here. See, but Indians don't have nothing to do with the hotel. I think the owners just like the name."

He watched Vernice thinking about it sipping her toddy, then begin to nod. "You're gonna tell this hotshot from Atlantic City you're a Chickasaw Indian—"

"I am, honey, part. I've told you that."

"And you expect having a few drops of Indian blood'll get you a job—I mean, a position?"

"I find out this fella has run a sports book, loves the game of baseball and has a head fulla stats. What I'm saying, I expect he could also know *me*."

"You're kidding," Vernice said, "aren't you?"

Being hurtful now as well as ignorant. It gave Charlie that urge to bear down and he said off the top of his head, "I'll bet you anything you want I get the job. How much?"

Vernice smiled, but it was like she felt sorry for him. She said, "Charlie, you ever get hired as a celebrity host I'll lose twenty pounds and go to work as a keno runner."

Sitting there like a strawberry sundae in her La-Z-Boy, knees apart—the woman's know-it-all tone of voice moved his irritation up a couple of notches and he said, "I was you, honey, I'd make it forty pounds."

She was having fun now and ignored the remark. "You're gonna tell this man you're a full-blooded Chickasaw."

"And played ball."

"Gonna paint your face and put on a war bonnet?"

"No," Charlie said, "I'm gonna tell this fella runs the place I'm a direct descendant of the man they named it for, Tishomingo himself."

Vernice said, "And you know what he'll say?"

He said, "Well, Chief, if I thought it mattered, can you prove it?"

This was in front of the Tishomingo Hotel & Casino as Billy Darwin came out of his Jaguar in leisure attire and Charlie introduced himself.

"During my playing days," Charlie said, "the *Tishomingo Times* in Oklahoma'd run stories about me and mention my lineage. I never left Tishomingo County till I was signed by the Baltimore organization."

"You played ball, uh?"

"Eighteen years. I phoned for an appointment, your girl put me down for two P.M. So while I been waiting an hour and a half," Charlie said, trying not to sound too irritated, "I been studying your tepee"—the three stories of concrete coming to a point above the entrance—"trying to think if Chickasaws ever lived in tepees, with or without all different-colored neon running up it, and it come to me that we never did."

Billy Darwin said, "That's what you want to see me about?"

"I thought I'd mention it. No, I'm here seeking employment as a celebrity host."

"As a relative of Tishomingo or a former ballplayer?"

"I can handle either, talk the talk."

When Billy Darwin shrugged and walked away, going into the hotel, Charlie was right behind him, passing through a room the size of a ballpark where they were laying carpet. On the escalator going up to the mezzanine Charlie said to the back of the man's silky sportshirt, "I was with five major-league organizations and pitched in a World Series."

Billy Darwin tossed his Robert Redford hair and looked over his shoulder as he reached the mezzanine.

"What year?"

"Eighty-four."

"Tigers over the Padres in five," Darwin said.

He kept walking and Charlie followed him through a reception area walled with murals, Plains Indians and buffalo, where some guys in suits were waiting, looking up to be noticed as Darwin went past, now into an office where a good-looking dark-haired woman sat behind a desk. Darwin stopped to ask her, "Carla, who was my two o'clock?"

She looked down at her pad and said, "Mr. Charlie Hoke. He wanted me to note, 'Former big leaguer.'"

Darwin turned enough to look at Charlie. "How do you spell your name?"

Charlie told him.

Darwin said, "You sure it's not H-o-a-x?"

Charlie said, "Billy"—hanging on to his irritation— "while you were playing stickball in the alley I was with the Orioles, the Texas Rangers, the Pittsburgh Pirates, the De-troit Tigers, Baltimore again, got traded back to De-troit in '83 and finished my eighteen years of organized ball with the Tigers in the '84 World Series. I went in what became the fi-nal game in the fifth and struck out the side. I got Brown and Salazar on called third strikes. I hit Wiggins by mistake, put him on, and I got the mighty Tony Gwynn to go down swing-ing at sixty-mile-an-hour knucklers. I went two and a third innings, threw twenty-six pitches and only five of 'em were balls. I hit Wiggins on a nothin'-and-two count, my only mistake, went to shave him with a fastball and come a little too close. I've struck out Al Oliver, Gorman Thomas and Jim Rice. Also Darrel Evans, Mike Schmidt, Bill Madlock, Willie McGee, Don Mattingly, and I fanned Wade Boggs twice in the same game—if those names mean anything to you."

Billy Darwin said, "Come on in," and led Charlie into an office big enough to hold a dance in and not even remove the desk, which by itself was a size. Darwin took his place behind it and began fooling with his computer, working the mouse, the PC and a phone the only things on the desk. Charlie got tired of standing and took one of the ranch-house leather chairs without being asked. Looking at Darwin close he saw the man was about forty, had that young-looking hair and appeared to be in shape. Charlie heard the computer making different noises like static on a radio, then was quiet and pretty soon Darwin went to work on the keyboard, typing and looking at the screen, which Charlie couldn't see.

He finally asked Darwin what he was doing and was told, "Looking you up on CNNSI dot com."

"I'm in there?"

"It says you're six-five and weigh two-twenty."

"I've shrunk," Charlie said. "I'm only six-four now."

"But you've put on some weight."

"Couple pounds."

Darwin was looking at the screen again. "The year you were with Detroit . . ." He stopped. "You only pitched those two and a third innings, allowed one hit, struck out five and walked two." The man sounding surprised as he read it off the screen.

"I only walked one. I told you I hit Wiggins? Come inside on him too close. See, I was never afraid to throw inside. You'd see these batters sticking their butts out ready to bail."

"But the only time you went up to the majors," Darwin said, "was in '84."

"I was up with other clubs but never used."

"And the only game you pitched in," Darwin said, "was in the World Series," the man still sounding surprised. "When did you strike out Mattingly, Madlock, all those guys you mentioned, Gorman Thomas?"

"You want," Charlie said, "I can go down the list. I got Mattingly when I was with Toledo in Triple-A and Don was with Columbus then. I recall I was playing A ball with Tulsa, a game against Shreveport I got Darrel Evans swinging. Madlock, let's see, I was with Oneonta, that's also A ball, and I believe he was with Pittsfield. I know Mike Schmidt was with Reading when I fanned him and I was playing Double-A with Altoona, back then throwing ninety-nine-mile-an-hour fastballs. I also held the record in the Eastern League for hitting the most batters."

Billy Darwin didn't look surprised anymore, sitting there deadpan, like he was looking at all these baseball facts sliding around in his head.

"Eighty-one I was back with De-troit, sent down to the Mud Hens and struck out Willie McGee. As I recall he was with the Louisville Riverbats. Who else you want to know? Oh, and I was in that longest game ever played that went thirty-two innings. You ever hear of it?"

"Pawtucket and Rochester," Darwin said, "yeah, '81."

"You know your baseball. Baltimore was giving me another shot, this time with Rochester, Triple-A, and I struck out Wade Boggs both times I faced him. The game lasted eight hours and seven minutes before they called it at four-oh-seven the next morning, Easter Sunday. Guys came home and caught hell, their wives thinking they were out all night fooling around."

"They finished the game sometime in June," Darwin said, "but I don't recall who won."

"I don't either," Charlie said. "I was gone by then." He grinned at Darwin. "I remember Wade Boggs saying, 'A game like this, you can have a bad week in one night.'"

Darwin was staring at him again and Charlie put on a serious look as Darwin said, "You spent your entire fucking career in the minors except for one game."

"I was up by the end of August that time. With other clubs too, but was mostly used for batting practice. I had all the pitches, even a split-finger that worked sometimes. I'd throw knucklers, give the boys a chance to see if they could hit junk. Or I'd come inside hard, get 'em to develop the nerve to hang in there."

"You were up several times—why didn't you ever stay?"

"I was wild my first, say, five years, I have to admit that. But being a southpaw with a blazing fastball, shit, there was always a club wanted to have a look at me. Then there was a period I might've been cuttin' up too much. I was having fun. Wherever I was I got my picture in the paper for one thing or another, like brawls they'd say I started. I'd hit a batter and he'd stand there giving me the evil eye. What I'd do, I'd hold my glove down by my leg and give him a motion with it like I'm saying, 'Come on. You think I hit you on purpose?' He'd come tearing at me and the benches'd empty. Seventy-three, or it might've been '74, I won the big-league bubble-gum-blowing contest." Charlie raised his hands like he was holding a basketball. "Goddamn bubble was this big, I swear."

He knew he had Darwin's attention, the way the man was staring at him, but couldn't tell what he was thinking.

"On the road for something to do, I'd catch balls dropped from the roof of hotels—put on one of those big mitts catchers use for knuckleballers? It always drew a crowd, only management never cared for what they called showing off. That's the kind of thing I'd get sent down for—don't come back till you grow up."

"I got a guy," Darwin said, "wants to dive off the roof of the hotel. What you said reminded me. He calls up, says he's a professional high diver and wants to know how many floors we have. I told him seven. He goes, 'I'll dive off the roof into eight feet of water.' And he'll bring his own tank."

"I'd like to see that," Charlie said. "How much's he want?"

"Five bills to go off twice a day."

"Sounds cheap enough for a death-defying stunt."

"Said he worked in Acapulco."

"Shit, I'd hire him. He likes high risk, he's no doubt a gambler. Pay him and win it all back at your tables."

Charlie noticed Billy Darwin's keen, appraising look and pulled out another idea that might impress him. "Set up one of those radar guns they use to see how hard the ball's thrown? Put in a pitching rubber and a bull's-eye sixty feet six inches away, a buck a throw. Anybody can throw a hardball a hunnert miles an hour wins . . . how much would you say?"

"Ten grand," Darwin said without even thinking about it.

"You have that on a sign by the radar cage," Charlie said. "Another one, it says 'Beat the big leaguer and win a hunnert bucks.' These strong young boys come along and look me over. 'Hell, I can take that old man.' Five bucks a throw—you could make some money off me."

Darwin kept staring at him. "You can still throw?"

"I can get it up to around eighty."

"Come on—an old guy like you?"

"Hell, I'm only fifty."

Darwin looked at his screen again. "Born in August of '48, you're pushing fifty-four."

"I can still throw harder'n most anybody wants to try me."

"You think," Darwin said, "you could strike me out?"

"You play much?"

"High school and sandlot, couple years of industrial ball."

"You bat right or left?"

"Left."

"Yeah, I can strike you out."

Darwin paused, thoughtful, and then asked him, "What've you been doing the past sixteen years?"

"I was a rep for the Jack Daniel's people, went on the road with promotions. Then did the same thing for Miller Brewing."

"You married?"

"Divorced, a long time. I have a couple of daughters, both in Florida, five grandchildren." Charlie said, "Is this the job interview?"

Darwin had that thoughtful look again. "You really think you can strike me out?"

Charlie shrugged this time. "Step up to the plate, we'll find out. You want to put money on it?"

The man kept staring. Finally he said, "How about this? I whiff, you're my celebrity host."

Charlie jumped on it. He said, "Hell, I'll strike you out on three pitches," and wanted to snatch the words back as he heard them. He saw Darwin smiling for the first time.

"I'll bet it was your mouth," Billy Darwin said, "kept you in the minors more'n your control." Not a half hour with

Charlie Hoke and starting to sound like him a little. Darwin said, "You're a gamer, Charlie. I'll give you four pitches."

Charlie set it up. He called Vernice at the Isle of Capri coffee shop, told her please not to ask any questions and let him talk to Lamont, one of the busboys. Lamont Harris was the catcher on the Rosa Fort high school baseball team. Charlie knew him from going over there this past spring to help the pitchers with their mechanics, hit fungoes and throw batting practice now and then. He told Lamont to meet them at the field after work, bring a couple of bats, a glove, his equipment and, hey, the oversized catcher's mitt Charlie had sold him for ten bucks.

By five-thirty they were out on the school's hardpack diamond playing catch. Charlie took his warm-up pitches, throwing mostly sliders and knucklers, while Billy Darwin in his sunglasses, shorts, his silky shirt and sneakers stood off to the side watching and swinging a bat. Lamont strapped on his protection and Charlie motioned him out to the mound. He told Lamont, a big seventeen-year-old he'd played catch with all spring, "Use the knuckleball mitt."

"That's all you gonna throw?"

"He'll think it and want to look the first one over. While he's looking," Charlie said, "I'm gonna throw it down the middle of downtown."

And that's what he did, grooved it. With that popping sound of the ball hitting the catcher's mitt, Lamont called,

"That's a strike," and Darwin turned his head to look at him. When he was facing this way again, swinging the bat out to point it at him, Charlie said, "You satisfied with the call?"

"It was a strike," Billy Darwin said, swung the bat out again, brought it back and dug in, Charlie observing the way he crowded the plate.

This time Charlie threw a slider, a two-bit curveball that came inside and hooked down and over the plate and Darwin swung late and missed. But he hung in, didn't he?

Okay, with the count nothing and two Charlie was thinking about offering a big, sweeping curve, lefty against lefty, throw it behind him and watch him hunch and duck as the ball broke over home plate. Or, hell, give him a knuckler, a pitch he'd likely never see. Get it anywhere near the plate he'll swing early and miss it a mile. Charlie gripped the ball with the tips of his gnarled fingers, his nails pressed into the hide, went into his motion, threw the floater and watched Darwin check his swing as the goddamn ball bounced a foot and a half in front of the plate.

"He came around on it," Charlie said.

Lamont was shaking his head saying no, he held up.

"We don't have a third base ump to call it," Charlie said, "but I'm pretty sure he came around."

Billy Darwin said, "Hey, Charlie, you threw it in the dirt, man. Come on, throw me a strike."

Shit.

What he needed was a resin bag.

Darwin was swinging the bat now and pointing it way out past Charlie toward the Mississippi River, then took his stance, digging in, and Charlie wasn't sure what to throw him. Maybe another slider, put it on the inside corner. Or show him a major-league fastball—or what passed for one sixteen years later. Shit. He felt his irritation heating up and told himself to throw the goddamn ball, fire it in there, this guy won't hit it, look at him holding the bat straight up behind him, waving the fat end in a circle. Jesus, a red bat, one of those metal ones they used in high school. You can't strike out a guy waving a tin bat at you, for Christ sake? Charlie went into his motion and bore down, threw it as hard as he could and saw the red bat fly up in the air as Billy Darwin hit the dirt to save his life.

Vernice, making the toddies this evening, said, "I don't understand why you threw it at him."

"I didn't; it got away from me is all. I should've taken time to settle down, talk to myself."

"But you lost your temper," Vernice said, handing Charlie his drink, "and your chance of getting that position."

"I ain't finished the story," Charlie said, in the La-Z-Boy where Vernice in her sympathy had let him sit. "I started toward him as he's brushing himself off. He says to me, picking up the bat, to stay out there and you bet I stopped in my tracks, in my goddamn wing tips. Now he's swinging the bat to show me where he wants it, belt-high, and says, 'Lay one in right here.' "

Vernice said, "He wasn't sore at you?"

"Lemme finish, okay? I laid one in and he hit it a mile out to right center. He says, 'There. Just so you know I can hit a baseball.' Then he says, 'You own a suit?' I told him of course

I owned a suit. He says, 'Put it on the day we open, and wear a tie.' "

Vernice seemed puzzled. "He hired you?"

"Yes, he did."

"Even though you knocked him down?"

Charlie said to her, "Honey, it's part of the game."

WHEN THE WOMEN
COME OUT TO DANCE

L ourdes became Mrs. Mahmood's personal maid when her friend Viviana quit to go to L.A. with her husband. Lourdes and Viviana were both from Cali in Colombia and had come to South Florida as mail-order brides. Lourdes' husband, Mr. Zimmer, worked for a paving contractor until his death, two years from the time they were married.

She came to the home on Ocean Drive, only a few blocks from Donald Trump's, expecting to not have a good feeling for a woman named Mrs. Mahmood, wife of Dr. Wasim Mahmood, who altered the faces and breasts of Palm Beach ladies and aspirated their areas of fat. So it surprised Lourdes the woman didn't look like a Mrs. Mahmood, and that she opened the door herself: this tall redheaded woman in a little green two-piece swimsuit, sunglasses on her nose, opened the door and said, "Lourdes, as in Our Lady of?"

"No, ma'am, Lour-des, the Spanish way to say it," and had to ask, "You have no help here to open the door?"

The redheaded Mrs. Mahmood said, "They're in the laundry room watching soaps." She said, "Come on in," and brought Lourdes into this home of marble floors, of statues and paintings that held no meaning, and out to the swimming pool, where they sat at a patio table beneath a yellow-and-white umbrella.

There were cigarettes, a silver lighter and a tall glass with only ice left in it on the table. Mrs. Mahmood lit a cigarette, a long Virginia Slim, and pushed the pack toward Lourdes, who was saying, "All I have is this, Mrs. Mahmood," Lourdes bringing a biographical data sheet, a printout, from her straw bag. She laid it before the redheaded woman showing her breasts as she leaned forward to look at the sheet.

" 'Your future wife is in the mail'?"

"From the Latina introduction list for marriage," Lourdes said. "The men who are interested see it on their computers. Is three years old, but what it tells of me is still true. Except of course my age. Now it would say thirty-five."

Mrs. Mahmood, with her wealth, her beauty products, looked no more than thirty. Her red hair was short and reminded Lourdes of the actress who used to be on TV at home, Jill St. John, with the same pale skin. She said, "That's right, you and Viviana were both mail-order brides," still looking at the sheet. "Your English is good—that's true. You don't smoke or drink."

"I drink now sometime, socially."

"You don't have e-mail."

"No, so we wrote letters to correspond, before he came to Cali, where I lived. They have parties for the men who come and we get—you know, we dress up for it."

"Look each other over."

"Yes, is how I met Mr. Zimmer in person."

"Is that what you called him?"

"I didn't call him anything."

"Mrs. Zimmer," the redheaded woman said. "How would you like to be Mrs. Mahmood?"

"I wouldn't think that was your name."

She was looking at the printout again. "You're virtuous, sensitive, hardworking, optimistic. Looking for a man who's a kind, loving person with a good job. Was that Mr. Zimmer?"

"He was okay except when he drank too much. I had to be careful what I said or it would cause him to hit me. He was strong, too, for a guy his age. He was fifty-eight."

"When you married?"

"When he died."

"I believe Viviana said he was killed?" The woman sounding like she was trying to recall whatever it was Viviana had told her. "An accident on the job?"

Lourdes believed the woman already knew about it, but said, "He was disappeared for a few days until they find his mix truck out by Hialeah, a pile of concrete by it but no reason for the truck to be here since there's no job he was pouring. So the police have the concrete broken open and find Mr. Zimmer."

"Murdered," the redheaded woman said.

"They believe so, yes, his hands tied behind him."

"The police talk to you?"

"Of course. He was my husband."

"I mean did they think you had anything to do with it."

She knew. Lourdes was sure of it.

"There was a suspicion that friends of mine here from Colombia could be the ones did it. Someone who was their enemy told this to the police."

"It have anything to do with drugs?"

The woman seeing all Colombians as drug dealers.

"My husband drove a cement truck."

"But why would anyone want to kill him?"

"Who knows?" Lourdes said. "This person who finked, he told the police I got the Colombian guys to do it because my husband was always beating me. One time he hit me so hard," Lourdes said, touching the strap of her blue sundress that was faded almost white from washing, "it separated my shoulder, the bones in here, so I couldn't work."

"Did you tell the Colombian guys he was beating you?"

"Everyone knew. Sometime Mr. Zimmer was brutal to me in public, when he was drinking."

"So maybe the Colombian guys did do it." The woman sounding like she wanted to believe it.

"I don't know," Lourdes said, and waited to see if this was the end of it. Her gaze moved out to the sunlight, to the water in the swimming pool lying still, and beyond to red bougainvillea growing against white walls. Gardeners were weeding and trimming, three of them Lourdes thought at first were Latino. No, the color of their skin was different. She said, "Those men . . ."

"Pakistanis," Mrs. Mahmood said.

"They don't seem to work too hard," Lourdes said. "I always have a garden at home, grow things to eat. Here, when I was married, I worked for Miss Olympia. She call her service 'Cleaning with Biblical Integrity.' I wasn't sure what it means, but she would say things to us from the Holy Bible. We cleaned offices in buildings in Miami. What I do here Viviana said would be different, personal to you. See to your things, keep your clothes nice?"

Straighten her dresser drawers. Clean her jewelry. Mrs. Mahmood said she kicked her shoes off in the closet, so Lourdes would see they were paired and hung in the shoe racks. Check to see what needed to be dry-cleaned. Lourdes waited as the woman stopped to think of other tasks. See to her makeup drawers in the bathroom. Lourdes would live here, have Sundays off, a half day during the week. Technically she would be an employee of Dr. Mahmood's.

Oh? Lourdes wasn't sure what that meant. Before she could ask, Mrs. Mahmood wanted to know if she was a naturalized citizen. Lourdes told her she was a permanent resident, but now had to get the papers to become a citizen.

"I say who I work for I put Dr. Wasim Mahmood?"

The redheaded wife said, "It's easier that way. You know, to handle what's taken out. But I'll see that you clear at least three-fifty a week."

Lourdes said that was very generous. "But will I be doing things also for Dr. Mahmood?"

The redheaded woman smoking her cigarette said, "What did Viviana tell you about him?"

"She say only that he didn't speak to her much."

"Viviana's a size twelve. Woz likes them young and as lean as snakes. How much do you weigh?"

"Less than one hundred twenty-five pounds."

"But not much—you may be safe. You cook?"

"Yes, of course."

"I mean for yourself. We go out or order in from restaurants. I won't go near that fucking stove and Woz knows it."

Lourdes said, "Wos?"

"Wasim. He thinks it's because I don't know how to cook, which I don't, really, but that's not the reason. The two regular maids are Filipina and speak English. In fact they have less of an accent than you. They won't give you any trouble, they look at the ground when they talk to anyone. And they leave at four, thank God. Woz always swims nude—don't ask me why, it might be a Muslim thing—so if they see him in the pool they hide in the laundry room. Or if I put on some Southern hip-hop and they happen to walk in while I'm bouncing to Dirty South doing my aerobics, they run for the laundry room." She said without a pause, "What did Viviana say about me?"

"Oh, how nice you are, what a pleasure to work here."

"Come on—I know she told you I was a stripper."

"She say you were a dancer before, yes."

"I started out in a dump on Federal Highway, got discovered and jumped to Miami Gold on Biscayne, valet parking. I was one of the very first, outside of black chicks, to do Southern hip-hop, and I mean Dirty South raw and uncut, while the other girls are doing Limp Bizkit, even some old Bob Seeger and Bad Company—and that's okay, whatever works for you. But in the meantime I'm making more doing laptops and private gigs than any girl at the Gold and I'm twenty-seven at the time, older than any of them. Woz would come in with his buddies, all suits and ties, trying hard not to look Third World. The first time he waved a fifty at me I gave him some close-up tribal strip-hop. I said, 'Doctor, you can see better if you put your eyeballs back in your head.' He loved that kind of talk. About the fourth visit I gave him what's known as the million-dollar hand job and became Mrs. Mahmood."

She told this sitting back relaxed, smoking her Virginia Slim cigarette, Lourdes nodding, wondering at times what she was talking about, Lourdes saying "I see" in a pleasant voice when the woman paused.

Now she was saying, "His first wife stayed in Pakistan while he was here in med school. Right after he finished his residency and opened his practice, she died." The woman said, "Let's see . . . You won't have to wear a uniform unless Woz wants you to serve drinks. Once in a while he has some of his ragtop buddies over for cocktails. Now you see these guys in their Nehru outfits and hear them chattering away in Urdu. I walk in, 'Ah, Mrs. Mahmood,' in that semi-British singsongy way they speak, 'what a lovely sight you are to my eyes this evening.' Wondering if I'm the same chick he used to watch strip."

She took time to light another cigarette and Lourdes said, "Do I wear my own clothes working here?"

"At first, but I'll get you some cool outfits. What are you, about an eight?"

"My size? Yes, I believe so."

"Let's see—stand up."

Lourdes rose and moved away from the table in the direction Mrs. Mahmood waved her hand. Now the woman was staring at her. She said, "I told you his first wife died?"

"Yes, ma'am, you did."

"She burned to death."

Lourdes said, "Oh?"

But the redheaded woman didn't tell her how it happened. She smoked her cigarette and said, "Your legs are good, but you're kinda short-waisted, a bit top-heavy. But don't worry, I'll get you fixed up. What's your favorite color?"

"I always like blue, Mrs. Mahmood."

She said, "Listen, I don't want you to call me that anymore. You can say ma'am in front of Woz to get my attention, but when it's just you and I? I'd rather you called me by my own name."

"Yes?"

"It's Ginger. Well, actually it's Janeen, but all of my friends call me Ginger. The ones I have left."

Meaning, Lourdes believed, since she was married to the doctor, friends who also danced naked, or maybe even guys.

Lourdes said, "Ginger?"

"Not Yinyor. Gin-ger. Try it again."

"Gin-gar?"

"That's close. Work on it."

But she could not make herself call Mrs. Mahmood Ginger. Not yet. Not during the first few weeks. Not on the shopping trip to Worth Avenue where Mrs. Mahmood knew everyone, all the salesgirls, and some of them did call her Ginger. She picked out for Lourdes casual summer dresses that cost hundreds of dollars each and some things from Resort Wear saying, "This is cute," and would hand it to the salesgirl to put aside, never asking Lourdes her opinion, if she liked the clothes or not. She did, but wished some of them were blue. Everything was yellow or yellow and white or white with yellow. She didn't have to wear a uniform, no, but now she matched the yellow-and-white patio, the cushions, the umbrellas, feeling herself part of the décor, invisible.

Sitting out here in the evening several times a week when the doctor didn't come home, Mrs. Mahmood trying hard to make it seem they were friends, Mrs. Mahmood serving daiquiris in round crystal goblets, waiting on her personal maid. It was nice to be treated this way and it would continue, Lourdes believed, until Mrs. Mahmood finally came out and said what was on her mind, what she wanted Lourdes to do for her.

The work was nothing, keep the woman's clothes in order, water the houseplants, fix lunch for herself—and the maids, once they came in the kitchen sniffing her spicy seafood dishes. Lourdes had no trouble talking to them. They looked right at her face telling her things. Why they avoided Dr. Mahmood. Because he would ask very personal questions about their sexual lives. Why they thought Mrs. Mahmood was crazy. Because of the way she danced in just her underwear.

And in the evening the woman of the house would tell Lourdes of being bored with her life, not able to invite her friends in because Woz didn't approve of them.

"What do I do? I hang out. I listen to music. I discuss soap operas with the gook maids. Melda stops me. 'Oh, missus, come quick.' They're in the laundry room watching *As the World Turns*. She goes, 'Dick follows Nikki to where she is to meet Ryder, and it look like he was going to hurt her. But Ryder came there in time to save Nikki from a violent Dick.' "

Mrs. Mahmood would tell a story like that and look at her

without an expression on her face, waiting for Lourdes to smile or laugh. But what was funny about the story?

"What do I do?" was the question she asked most. "I exist, I have no life."

"You go shopping."

"That's all."

"You play golf."

"You've gotta be kidding."

"You go out with your husband."

"To an Indian restaurant and I listen to him talk to the manager. How many times since you've been here has he come home in the evening? He has a girlfriend," the good-looking redheaded woman said. "He's with her all the time. Her or another one, and doesn't care that I know. He's rubbing it in my face. All guys fool around at least once in a while. Woz and his buddies live for it. It's accepted over there, where they're from. A guy gets tired of his wife in Pakistan? He burns her to death. Or has it done. I'm not kidding, he tells everyone her *dupatta* caught fire from the stove."

Lourdes said, "Ah, that's why you don't cook."

"Among other reasons. Woz's from Rawalpindi, a town where forty women a *month* show up at the hospital with terrible burns. If the woman survives . . . Are you listening to me?"

Lourdes was sipping her daiquiri. "Yes, of course."

"If she doesn't die, she lives in shame because her husband, this prick who tried to burn her to death, kicked her out of the fucking house. And he gets away with it. Pakistan, India, thousands of women are burned every year 'cause their husbands are tired of them, or they didn't come up with a big enough dowry."

"You say the first wife was burn to death."

"Once he could afford white women—like, what would he need her for?"

"You afraid he's going to burn you?"

"It's what they do, their custom. And you know what's ironic? Woz comes here to be a plastic surgeon, but over in Pakistan, where all these women are going around disfigured? There are no plastic surgeons to speak of." She said, "Some of them get acid thrown in their face." She said, "I made the biggest mistake of my life marrying a guy from a different culture, a towelhead."

Lourdes said, "Why did you?"

She gestured. "This . . ." Meaning the house and all that went with it.

"So you have what you want."

"I won't if I leave him."

"Maybe in the divorce he let you keep the house."

"It's in the prenup, I get zip. And at thirty-two I'm back stripping on Federal Highway, or working in one of those top-less doughnut places. You have tits, at least you can get a job. Woz's favorite, I'd come out in a nurse's uniform, peel everything off but the perky little cap?" The woman's mind moving to this without pausing. "Woz said the first time he saw the act he wanted to hire me. I'd be the first topless surgical nurse."

Lourdes imagined this woman dancing naked, men watching her, and thought of Miss Olympia warning the cleaning women with her Biblical Integrity: no singing or dancing around while cleaning the offices, or they might catch the eye of men working late. She made it sound as if they were lying in wait. "Read the Book of Judges," Miss Olympia said, "the twenty-first verse." It was about men waiting for women, the daughters of Shiloh, to come out to dance so they could take them, force the women to be their wives. Lourdes knew of cleaning women who sang while they worked, but not ones who danced. She wondered what it would be like to dance naked in front of men.

"You don't want to be with him," Lourdes said, "but you want to live in this house."

"There it is," the woman who didn't look at all like a Mrs. Mahmood said.

Lourdes sipped her daiquiri, put the glass down and reached for the pack of Virginia Slims on the table.

"May I try one of these?"

"Help yourself."

She lit the cigarette, sucking hard to get a good draw. She said, "I use to smoke. The way you do it made me want to smoke again. Even the way you hold the cigarette."

Lourdes believed the woman was very close to telling what she was thinking about. Still, it was not something easy to talk about with another person, even for a woman who danced naked. Lourdes decided this evening to help her.

She said, "How would you feel if a load of wet concrete fell on your husband?"

Then wondered, sitting in the silence, not looking at the woman, if she had spoken too soon.

The redheaded woman said, "The way it happened to Mr. Zimmer? How did you feel?"

"I accepted it," Lourdes said, "with a feeling of relief, knowing I wouldn't be beaten no more."

"Were you ever happy with him?"

"Not for one day."

"You picked him, you must've had some idea."

"He picked me. At the party in Cali? There were seven Colombian girls for each American. I didn't think I would be chosen. We married . . . In two years I had my green card and was tired of him hitting me."

The redheaded Mrs. Mahmood said, "You took a lot of shit, didn't you?" and paused this time before saying, "How much does a load of concrete cost these days?"

Lourdes, without pausing, said, "Thirty thousand."

Mrs. Mahmood said, "Jesus Christ," but was composed, sitting back in her yellow cushions. She said, "You were ready. Viviana told you the situation and you decided to go for it."

"I think it was you hired me," Lourdes said, "because of Mr. Zimmer—you so interested in what happen to him. Also I could tell, from the first day we sat here, you don't care for your husband."

"You can understand why, can't you? I'm scared to death of catching on fire. He lights a cigar, I watch him like a fucking hawk."

Giving herself a reason, an excuse.

"We don't need to talk about him," Lourdes said. "You pay the money, all of it before, and we don't speak of this again. You don't pay, we still never speak of it."

"The Colombian guys have to have it all up front?"

"The what guys?"

"The concrete guys."

"You don't know what kind of guys they are. What if it

looks like an accident and you say oh, they didn't do nothing, he fell off his boat."

"Woz doesn't have a boat."

"Or his car was hit by a truck. You understand? You not going to know anything before."

"I suppose they want cash."

"Of course."

"I can't go to the bank and draw that much."

"Then we forget it."

Lourdes waited while the woman thought about it smoking her Virginia Slim, both of them smoking, until Mrs. Mahmood said, "If I give you close to twenty thousand in cash, today, right now, you still want to forget it?"

Now Lourdes had to stop and think for a moment.

"You have that much in the house?"

"My getaway money," Mrs. Mahmood said, "in case I ever have to leave in a hurry. What I socked away in tips getting guys to spot their pants and that's the deal, twenty grand. You want it or not? You don't, you might as well leave, I don't need you anymore."

So far in the few weeks she was here, Lourdes had met Dr. Mahmood face-to-face with reason to speak to him only twice. The first time, when he came in the kitchen and asked her to prepare his breakfast, the smoked snook, a fish he ate cold with tea and whole wheat toast. He asked her to have some of the snook if she wished, saying it wasn't as good as kippers but would do. Lourdes tried a piece;

it was full of bones but she told him yes, it was good. They spoke of different kinds of fish from the ocean they liked and he seemed to be a pleasant, reasonable man.

The second time Lourdes was with him face-to-face he startled her, coming out of the swimming pool naked as she was watering the plants on the patio. He called to her to bring him his towel from the chair. When she came with it he said, "You were waiting for me?"

"No, sir, I didn't see you."

As he dried his face and his head, the hair so short it appeared shaved, she stared at his skin, at his round belly and his strange black penis, Lourdes looking up then as he lowered the towel.

He said, "You are a widow?" She nodded yes and he said, "When you married, you were a virgin?"

She hesitated, but then answered because she was telling a doctor, "No, sir."

"It wasn't important to your husband."

"I don't think so."

"Would you see an advantage in again being a virgin?"

She had to think—it wasn't something ever in her mind before—but didn't want to make the doctor wait, so she said, "No, not at my age."

The doctor said, "I can restore it if you wish."

"Make me a virgin?"

"Surgically, a few sutures down there in the tender dark. It's becoming popular in the Orient with girls entering marriage. Also for prostitutes. They can charge much more, often thousands of dollars for that one night." He said, "I'm thinking of offering the procedure. Should you change your mind, wish me to examine you, I could do it in your room."

Dr. Mahmood's manner, and the way he looked at her that time, made Lourdes feel like taking her clothes off.

He didn't come home the night Lourdes and Mrs. Mahmood got down to business. Or the next night. The morning of the following day, two men from the Palm Beach County sheriff's office came to the house. They showed Lourdes their identification and asked to see Mrs. Mahmood.

She was upstairs in her bedroom trying on a black dress, looking at herself in the full-length mirror and then at Lourdes' reflection appearing behind her.

"The police are here," Lourdes said.

Mrs. Mahmood nodded and said, "What do you think?" turning to pose in the dress, the skirt quite short.

Lourdes read the story in the newspaper that said Dr. Wasim Mahmood, prominent etc., etc., had suffered gunshot wounds during an apparent carjacking on Flagler near Currie Park and was pronounced dead on arrival at Good Samaritan. His Mercedes was found abandoned on the street in Delray Beach.

Mrs. Mahmood left the house in her black dress. Later, she phoned to tell Lourdes she had identified the body, spent time with the police, who had no clues, nothing at all to go on, then stopped by a funeral home and arranged to have Woz cremated without delay. She said, "What do you think?"

"About what?" Lourdes said.

"Having the fucker burned."

She said she was stopping to see friends and wouldn't be home until late.

One A.M., following an informal evening of drinks with old friends, Mrs. Mahmood came into the kitchen from the garage and began to lose her glow.

What was going on here?

Rum and mixes on the counter, limes, a bowl of ice. A Latin beat coming from the patio. She followed the sound to a ring of burning candles, to Lourdes in a green swimsuit moving in one place to the beat, hands raised, Lourdes grinding her hips in a subtle way.

The two guys at the table smoking cigarettes saw Mrs. Mahmood, but made no move to get up.

Now Lourdes turned from them and saw her, Lourdes smiling a little as she said, "How you doing? You look like you feeling no pain."

"You have my suit on," Mrs. Mahmood said.

"I put on my yellow one," Lourdes said, still moving in that subtle way, "and took it off. I don't wear yellow no more, so I borrow one of yours. Is okay, isn' it?"

Mrs. Mahmood said, "What's going on?"

"This is *cumbia,* Colombian music for when you want to celebrate. For a wedding, a funeral, anything you want. The candles are part of it. *Cumbia,* you should always light candles."

Mrs. Mahmood said, "Yeah, but what is going on?"

"We having a party for you, Ginger. The Colombian guys come to see you dance."

FIRE IN THE HOLE

I.

They had dug coal together as young men and then lost touch over the years. Now it looked like they'd be meeting again, this time as lawman and felon, Raylan Givens and Boyd Crowder.

Boyd did six years in a federal penitentiary for refusing to pay his income tax, came out and found religion. He received his ordination by mail order from a Bible college in South Carolina and formed a sect he called Christian Aggression. The next thing he did, Boyd formed the East Kentucky Militia with a cadre of neo-Nazi skinheads, a bunch of boys wearing Doc Martens and swastika tattoos. They were all natural-born racists and haters of authority, but still had to be taught what Boyd called "the laws of White Supremacy as laid down by the Lord," which he took from Christian Identity doctrines. Next thing, he trained these boys in the use of explosives and automatic weapons. He told them they were now members of Crowder's Commandos, sworn to take up the fight for freedom against the coming Mongrel World Order and the govermint's illegal tax laws.

Boyd said he would kill the next man tried to make him pay income tax.

The skinheads accepted Boyd as the real thing, his having seen combat. Boyd had caught the tail end of Vietnam, came back with three pairs of Charlie's ears on silver chains and an Air CAV insignia on his arm, the tat faded from having been there now some twenty-five years.

Raylan Givens, a few years younger than Boyd, was now a deputy United States marshal. Raylan was known as the one who'd shot it out with a Miami gangster named Tommy Bucks—also known as the Zip—both men seated at the same table in the dining area of the Cardozo Hotel, South Beach, when they drew their pistols. Raylan had told the Zip he had twenty-four hours to get out of Dade County or he would shoot him on sight. When the Zip failed to comply, Raylan kept his word, shot him through china and glassware from no more than six feet away.

The day the Marshals Service assigned Raylan to a Special Operations Group and transferred him from Florida to Harlan County, Kentucky, Boyd Crowder was on his way to Cincinnati to blow up the IRS office in the federal building.

II.

Boyd was making the run in a new Chevy Blazer, all mud from wheels to roof after coming out of the hollows and forks of East Kentucky. The Blazer belonged to his skinhead driver, a new boy named Jared who'd just finished his sixty-day basic training and indoctrination, a skinhead from Oklahoma. Boyd said to him, "You see where out'n Oregon a militia group threw a stink bomb in their IRS office?"

"A *stink* bomb," Jared said, his eyes holding on the road, the view all trees, sky and semis. He said, "Shit, throw a pipe bomb in there, a grenade, you want to get their attention."

It sounded good, but did he mean it? Boyd had his doubts about this Jared from Oklahoma.

They had come out of deep woods five hours ago and were now following 75 on its approach to Covington and the Ohio River. Riding with them in back, covered in plastic wrap, were a pair of Chinese AKs, ammo and an RPG-7 antitank grenade launcher, another Chink weapon Boyd had used in the Nam, a little honey that fired a 40-millimeter hollow-charge rocket grenade.

He said to Jared, "I want you to tell me if there's something you don't understand about what you been learning."

Jared moved his shoulders in kind of a shrug, eyes straight ahead as they came up on a line of big diesel haulers. He had that lazy manner skinheads put on to show they were cool. He said, "Well, a couple of things. I don't understand all that Christian Identity stuff, their calling Jews the progeny of Satan and niggers subhuman."

Boyd said, "Hell, it's right in the Bible, I'll show it to you we get back. Okay, what're the Jews behind?"

"They control the Federal Reserve."

"What else?"

Jared said, "ZOG?" not sounding too sure.

"You betcha ZOG, the Zionist Occupational Government," Boyd said, "the ones set to rule us we let the gover-mint take away our guns. You see Chuck Heston on TV? Chuck said they'd have to take his out of his cold dead hand."

"Yeah, I saw him," Jared said, not sounding moved or inspired. Then saying, "There's Cincinnati up ahead. You see it before you get to the bridge."

This Jared had come recommended from an Oklahoma group, the Aryan Knights of Freedom, Jared saying he heard of Crowder's Commandos he couldn't wait to drive his new SUV over to Kentucky and join up. Saying he was anxious to get into high explosives 'stead of chasing niggers down alleys and spray-painting synagogues; shit. He said he was in Oklahoma City for the Murrah Federal Building, got there just a few minutes after she blew. He said it had inspired him to get in the fight. Sometimes talking about the Murrah Building it would sound like he had taken part in that mission with Tim and Terry.

No, Boyd and others weren't all that sold on this Jared from Oklahoma. How come he didn't have any Aryan tattoos? How come he was always touching his head? Like wondering if his hair would ever grow in again. Boyd didn't personally care for that bare-skull look, but allowed it since it was what they were known as. He preferred an inch on top and shaved sidewalls like his own regulation grunt cut, now mostly gray at fifty, steel bristles crowning his lean leathery face.

They were coming on to Cincy now, its downtown standing over there against a sky losing its light. A few minutes later they were on the northbound span of the Ohio River bridge. Boyd said, "Get off on Fifth Street."

"Another thing I don't understand," Jared said, "there's all these white power outfits around but nothing holding 'em together, no kind of plan I ever heard of."

"Except purpose," Boyd said. "Militias, the Klan, your pissed-off Libertarians and tax protesters, your various Aryan brotherhoods, we're all part of the same patriot movement."

They were on Fifth now passing hotels and that big fountain there.

"Also you have your millions who don't even realize yet they're part of the revolution. I'm talking about all the people caught up in white flight. You know what that is?"

"Yes sir, people moving out of town."

"White people moving to the suburbs. You think it's 'cause they're dying to cut grass and have barbecues in the backyard? Shit no, it's to get away from the niggers and greasers. And Asiatics, Christ, we got 'em all. Anybody wants in, sure, come on. Look at all the fuckin' Mexicans . . ."

He paused to give directions, but Jared was already turning left onto Main—without being told where they were going, now or anytime before.

Boyd gave him a look, but then had to hunch down as they passed the John Weld Peck Federal Building, Boyd trying to see up to the seventh floor of the nine-story building, where the IRS office was located. All he saw was a wall of tall rectangular windows up no more than a few floors. Sitting up again Boyd said, "Take a left on Sixth and come around the block."

They passed the Subway sandwich shop on Sixth his recon man Devil Ellis had told him about. Boyd didn't mention it or say a word the rest of the way around the block, not until they were coming up on the federal building again.

"Lemme off on the corner over there and make your circle. I'll be waiting."

Jared turned left, pulled up in front of the yellow Subway awning, and Boyd got out. He went inside the shop—no one here but the woman behind the counter—and stood at the plate-glass window smelling onions. The view showed most of the John Weld Peck Building diagonally across the way. From here, Devil Ellis said, he'd have a clear shot at the corner windows up there. Which was how much Devil—what they called him—knew about firing a grenade rocket at a target this close and high up. It was the kind of stunt Devil would try, stoned or just crazy, stand here chewing on a roast beef sub dripping onions and decide, yeah, shoot through this big window.

Devil was the one drove down to the Tennessee line one night and set off a charge in the Jellico post office, and all the pissed-off retirees had to wait and wait to get their social security checks, which didn't help the cause. Got the post office bombing listed with the abortion clinic Boyd was supposed to have blown up—the dumbest thing he ever heard of. What did you gain by it? Rob a bank and spray-paint *White Power* on the wall, you make your point and get away with a bag or two of cash.

It was Devil told him to keep an eye on Jared—both Devil and Boyd's baby brother, Bowman, suspecting Jared had been planted among them by the FBI, the Federal Bureau of Imperialism, or was an agent himself, although pretty dumb.

Boyd walked out to the corner and stood watching for unmarked cars creeping around, vans parked where they shouldn't be, spotters inside. It was getting dark already.

The muddy Blazer rolled up. Boyd got in and Jared said, "Which way?"

"Straight ahead."

Boyd sat there and didn't speak again until they were up Main Street a ways, crossing East Central Parkway now, and Boyd said, "We coming to it, Niggaville," Boyd looking at dingy old buildings, run-down storefronts, people he saw as winos on the street. Another couple of blocks and he spotted the place Devil told him to look for. Sure enough, up on the right. "There it is," Boyd said. "Go past slow." He could read the sign now sticking out from the front of the building:

TEMPLE OF THE COOL AND BEAUTIFUL J.C.

A thin coat of whitewash covered the front, the place a dump, the sign blasphemous, calling Jesus cool and beautiful, for Christ sake.

"Turn left that next street and stop. I believe I can take 'er from over there." Boyd stuck his butt in Jared's face pushing his way between the seats to get in the back. Jared raising his voice now:

"You gonna blow up that church?" Sounding surprised, then in kind of a panic. "Boyd, we're in the middle of fucking Cincinnati."

Now Boyd, in the back end of the Blazer, getting his Chinese grenade launcher unwrapped, raised his own voice to tell Jared, "You always have a secondary target, just in case." He looked out the rear as Jared came to a stop. "This is good, I'm gonna have a clear shot."

"Boyd, there's people on the street."

"I don't see none. Just some niggers."

"They gonna *see* us. I.D. my *car*."

Boyd loved times like these he could show how cool he was under fire, so to speak. "You worried about your car, huh?"

"They's people right up the block, watching. Boyd, you see 'em? They watching us."

Even if this Jared wasn't a snitch, which could be, he sure as hell wasn't commando material. "Fuck 'em," Boyd said. "We're about to raise a whole lot of hell."

He had the RPG just about put together. He'd screwed the propellant cylinder to the back of the missile grenade and slipped it into the tube, sticking out now like a fat spear. Next, he removed the nose cap from it. Shit, he could do this in the dark drinking from a jar of shine. He pulled out the pin, the safety, and called to Jared to get ready.

Now Boyd dropped the tailgate and slipped out to the street with his rocket gun, hefted it to his shoulder, flipped the sight up and took aim. He called out to no one in particular, "Fire in the hole!" Squeezed the trigger and that Temple of the Cool and Beautiful J.C. blew up before his eyes.

III.

Boyd got rid of the RPG crossing the Ohio River south, stuck his head and shoulders out the back end of the vehicle and flung the weapon out into the night. He told Jared to look for 275. That took them over to the airport, where he got Jared to follow the signs to long-term parking and find a spot a good ways from the terminal. "Over there toward the fence," Boyd said, still crouched down in the back end.

Once they were parked, Jared said, "Now what?" sounding like all his energy had drained out of him.

Boyd didn't answer. He had one of the Chink AK-47s unwrapped and armed with a magazine. He heard in his mind the familiar words *lock and load* and was ready for business.

Jared said to the rearview mirror, "What're you doing?"

Boyd could see just the top of his head above the cushion on the front seat.

"How'd you know where we was going?"

"What?"

"You heard me." It was quiet in here, neither of them moving.

"How'd you know we's going to the federal building?"

Now Jared's voice in the dark said, "Was your brother told me. Him and Devil."

"You mean you heard 'em talking?"

"Uh-unh, Bowman told me and then Devil goes, 'But don't let on you know.' "

"I think you spied on 'em."

"No sir—you can ask 'em."

"I think you listen in on things you shouldn't, and then report it to who you work for. Is that what you are, a snitch for the feds?"

Jared had his head raised to the rearview mirror.

"Boyd, you got no reason to say that, none."

"I saw how you acted, I'm setting up to blow out that nigger church. You didn't want no parts of it."

"They was *people* around, watching us."

Sounding like he was starting to panic again. Boyd asked himself, You want to argue with him or get 'er done?

He laid the barrel of the assault rifle on the backrest of the seat close in front of him and *bam,* shot Jared through the headrest of the driver's seat—the round going through the fat cushion, through Jared, through the windshield, through the rear window of the car in front of the Blazer and through its windshield—Boyd discovering this once he was outside and took a look.

From the terminal he called Devil Ellis at the Sukey Ridge church to tell him he'd arrive at the London-Corbin airport on the late shuttle. Devil was full of questions on the phone, but Boyd managed to satisfy him with, "Yeah, I had to let Jared go. I'll tell you about it when you get me."

Now in Devil's pickup, trailing its headlights along pitch-dark roads toward Sukey Ridge, Boyd filled him in: how he'd knocked out the nigger church—Devil letting out a Rebel yell—and then how, not taking any chances, he shot Jared, wiped down the Blazer pretty good where he'd sat, and stashed the rifles and extra RPG loads and parts along that cyclone fence there separating the lot from the airfield? They'd send one of the skins, see if he could pick 'em up.

Boyd sipped from a jar Devil kept in his truck, then looked over at him with his dark beard and black cowpuncher hat Boyd allowed, the look being the man's style, Devil's devilish, go-to-hell image.

"Jared said you told him where we's going."

"Yeah, me and Bowman."

Boyd took another sip of the shine. "Even thinking he was a snitch?"

"Bowman figured Jared'd fuck up and you'd see he knew more'n he was supposed to and you'd get on him about it."

Boyd said, "Yeah . . . ?"

"Jared'd say it was us told him and you wouldn't believe it."

Boyd said, "Then what?"

"We figured you'd work on him in your way and get him to confess."

Boyd said, "That he's a traitorous snitch."

"Yeah, in the pay of the govermint."

"But he didn't tell me nothing like that."

"You work on him?"

"I started in but, hell, I knew he'd lie to me."

"I know what you mean—those people. So you put him down. I'd have done the same."

Boyd didn't say anything to that. They drove through the dark in silence till Devil said, "You know how he was always talking about the Murrah Building, saying he was there like a minute after she blew? Me and Bowman don't believe he was anywheres near it. Saw it on TV like everybody else."

Boyd said, "Was it you didn't trust him or you just didn't like him much?"

Devil said after a moment, "I guess both."

They were coming to the church now, way up there where that speck of electric light showed on the ridge. Across the front of the property, coming down to the dirt road they followed, was a pasture, a good five acres of cleared land and no road leading up. It was around the next bend where the pickup slowed to turn into the trees past the sign that said PRIVATE PROPERTY—TRESPASSERS WILL BE SHOT.

Boyd said, "You watching for claymores?"

"You think you're funny," Ellis said. "If I believed you planted any I'd move clear to Tennessee."

They followed switchbacks up through the trees finally to top a rise and coast into the barnlot back of the old church, not used for services since Ike was President. Boyd had bought it cheap, had it painted and turned into a dormitory for when his skinheads were here. Anybody complained it looked like a prison dorm, Boyd would tell 'em to go sleep in the barn—with a mean rat-eating owl lived there. He got out of the truck stiff, tired from riding.

Three skins watched him from the back porch where a kerosene lamp sat on top the fridge. The two fat boys were locals Boyd called the Pork brothers. The one without a shirt this cool evening, his dyed-blond hair spiked, was a boy named Dewey Crowe from Lake Okeechobee in Florida. He wore a necklace of alligator teeth along with the word HEIL tattooed on one tit and HITLER on the other, part of the Führer's name in the boy's armpit.

Walking toward them Boyd said, "What's going on?"

It was Dewey Crowe who spoke up. "Your brother got shot."

The words came at Boyd cold, without any note of sympathy, so he took it to mean Bowman wasn't shot any place'd kill him.

But then Dewey said, "He's dead," in that same flat tone of voice.

And it hit Boyd like a shock of electricity. Wait a minute—in his mind seeing his brother alive and in his prime, grown even bigger'n Boyd. How could he be dead?

"Was his wife shot him," Dewey said, "with his deer rifle. They say Ava done it while Bowman was having his supper."

IV.

It was Art Mullen, marshal in charge of this East Kentucky Special Op Group, who had requested Raylan Givens, now seated in Art's temporary office in the Harlan County courthouse. It was an overcast morning in October, the two sipping coffee, getting acquainted again.

"I remember you were from around here."

"A long time ago."

"You still look the same as you did at Glynco," Art said, meaning the time they were both firearms instructors at the academy. "Still wearing the dark suit and wing-tip cowboy boots."

"The boots're fairly new."

"Don't tell me that hat is." The kind Art Mullen thought of as a businessman's Stetson, except no businessman'd wear this one with its creases and just slightly curled brim cocked toward one eye, the hat part of Raylan's lawman personality. He said no, it was old.

"What do you pack these days?"

"This trip my old Smith forty-five Target." He saw Art grin.

"You and your big six-shooter—born a hundred years too late. You ever get married again?"

"No, but I wouldn't mind some homelife. I can't say

Winona ruined it for me. I stopped to see my two boys on the way up. They come down to Florida every summer and I get 'em jobs."

There was a lull. Raylan looked toward the gray sky in the window, trees starting to change color. Art Mullen, a big, comfortable man with a quiet way of speaking, said, "Tell me what you remember of Boyd Crowder."

Raylan, nodding his head a couple of times, went back to that time in his mind. "Well, we dug coal side by side for Eastover Mining, near Brookside. Boyd was a few years older and had become a powderman. He'd crawl down a hole with his case of Emulex five-twenty and come out stringing wire. You'd hear him call out 'Fire in the hole,' to clear the shaft. She'd blow and we'd go back in to dig out the pieces. We weren't what you'd call buddies, but you work a deep mine with a man you look out for each other."

Art Mullen said, "Fire in the hole, uh?" in a thoughtful kind of way.

"I hate to say he was good at it," Raylan said, and sipped his coffee, still back all those years in his mind. "I remember when we struck Eastover and Duke Power brought in scabs and gun thugs? Their cars'd drive in, Boyd'd be waiting to swing at 'em with a wrecking bar. He was put in jail twice. Then when he shot one of the scabs, almost killed him, Boyd took off and I heard he joined the army. Came out and what happened, he went to prison?"

"Came out pissing and moaning," Art said, " 'cause we quit in Vietnam 'stead of getting it done. He bought a truck and went to work hauling timber for the mines. Ten years never paid his income tax, refused to, claiming he was a sovereign citizen. The U.S. attorney sent him to Alderson. That's where he got into what they call the patriot movement. You read his sheet?"

"I've only had time to skim it so far," Raylan said. "He's been busy, huh? Has his own army now, bunch of serious morons sieg-heilin' each other?"

"More serious'n you think," Art said. "Boyd's got 'em making horseshit bombs, fertilizer and fuel oil. They drive to a town like Somerset, blow up somebody's car to get the police busy and go rob a bank."

Raylan was nodding. "I saw it in a Steve McQueen movie."

"Well, these people aren't movie actors." Art leaned forward, resting his arms on the desk. "Lemme tell you about this guy they found at the Cincinnati airport, sitting in his new Chevy Blazer shot through the back of the head. This is Jared, on file with the Bureau as some kind of Aryan knight. Oklahoma driver's license and registration."

"You put him with Boyd?"

"Lemme get to it," Art said. "This is good. Just the night before, a black church in Cincinnati—they called it a street mission in the paper—was blown up."

Raylan was frowning. "It was a church? I caught only part of it on the news."

Art held up one hand. "Listen to me. Four witnesses say a guy got out of the Blazer with what looked like a bazooka and fired it into the church. But right before, you know what he said, yelled it out? 'Fire in the hole.' "

Raylan straightened. He said, "Come on . . ." his interest picking up.

"All four witnesses heard it. So now evidence techs go

through the Blazer. They find this little cardboard cylinder you hook onto the back of an RPG rocket. It holds the juice, the propellant. One he must've missed."

"So you got the dead guy with Boyd."

"It would seem, huh? But first," Art said, "we want to put Boyd and the dead guy at the church. What's interesting, it's only kind of a church. The pastor, it turns out, Israel Fandi, is one of the witnesses. Only at first he won't admit who he is till people start pointing at him. Israel wears an African outfit, a dashiki and a little pillbox hat and talks like he's Rastafarian. You know what I mean?"

"Ethiopian," Raylan said. "By way of Jamaica. I remember now on the news they said it was believed the people smoked ganja as part of the service."

"They smoked it, they sold it—the place was a dope store passing as a church. It blew," Art said, "there was free grass all over the block. This was three days ago. Since then we got the Cincinnati police to loan us Israel Fandi. He's in a holding cell downstairs, but claims he didn't see the man's face had the bazooka. I said to him, 'Israel, you see him in a lineup, the man we *know* blew up your church, you might change your mind.'"

"The power of suggestion," Raylan said.

"Without holding the marijuana over his head. We'll save it. Next thing is to pick up Boyd, if he's still around."

"What've you got on him otherwise?"

"The U.S. attorney wants to collect indictments under a charge of sedition. That he did willfully and knowingly et cetera conspire to overthrow, put down and destroy by force the government of the United States."

"But what've you got you can take to court?"

"Only bits and pieces of evidence."

"Then he's most likely still around," Raylan said.

"Well, he's got sympathizers. Half the people living up in the hollers around here," Art said, "are on welfare but still don't trust the government, won't talk to census takers. Boyd's mother and his ex-wife are in Evarts. His skinheads train at a place up on Sukey Ridge, what he calls his Christian Aggression Church. Signs on the trees say you approach at your own risk, as the road's been mined."

"You let him get away with that?"

"ATF swept it. There aren't any mines. Another house, one he used to own up on Black Mountain? It's been under fore-closure since he went to prison. We want to sell it to cover his back taxes, but Boyd's put the word out, anybody buys the house, he'll blow it up."

"I remember," Raylan said, "they used to raise marijuana crops up there, acres of plants all the way down across the Vir-ginia line."

"They're still growing it, but that's not our business, bust-ing dopers."

"No, but what I was thinking," Raylan said, "Israel being into weed, what if you sold the house to him? Say for a hun-dred bucks or so." He had Art starting to grin. "And you let Boyd know a black guy's living in his house."

Not a bad idea, Art saying yeah, that could bring him out. Saying then, "There's another situation could do it. You know Bowman, Boyd's brother?"

Raylan saw him in a football uniform. "Sorta. He was a star running back in high school—this was after I got out. Boyd was always talking about him, how Bowman had the goods and would go on to play college ball and become a pro. I was never that sure."

Art said, "You remember the girl he married, Ava?"

Raylan's tone came alive as he said, "Ava, yeah, she lived down the street from us." He remembered her eyes. "She's married to Bowman?"

"Was," Art said. "She ended the union the other day with a thirty-ought-six, plugged him through the heart."

It stopped Raylan. He remembered a cute little dark-haired girl about sixteen and how she tried to act older, flirting, working her brown eyes on him. He remembered her sassy cheerleader moves on the field Friday nights, the girls in blue and gold doing their routines, and his eyes would be on Ava the whole time. Too young or he would've gone after her.

He said to Art, "You talk to her?"

"She admits shooting him. Ava said she got tired of him getting drunk and beating her up. She was arraigned this morning. Her lawyer had her plead not guilty to first and second degree and she was released on her own recognizance. Unusual, but the prosecutor, knowing Bowman, would just as soon not bring her up. They'll work out a plea deal."

"Where is she now?"

"Went home. I told her, you know Boyd's gonna come looking for you. She said it's none of our business. I told her it is if he shoots you. You want to talk to her?"

"I wouldn't mind," Raylan said.

V.

She'd be fixing her face to go to work at Betty's Hair Salon, and Bowman would say, "Who you think you are, Ava Gardner? You don't look nothing like her."

Ava had quit trying to get it through his head no one ever said she did. The day she was born her daddy named her Ava on account of Ava Gardner saying she was a country girl at heart with a country girl's values. He had read it somewhere and believed it and would remind her as she was growing up, "See, even a good-looking woman don't have to put on airs."

She married Bowman a year out of high school because he was cute, because he was sure of himself and told her he'd never work in a goddamn coal mine. He'd wear the blue and white of the University of Kentucky and after that get drafted by a pro team; he wouldn't mind the Cowboys. But colleges either wouldn't accept his grades or didn't think he was good enough. He blamed her for their getting married and taking his mind off staying in shape so he could try out at some school as a walk-on. She said, "Honey, if your grade-point average sucks . . ." Uh-unh, that had nothing to do with it, it was her fault. Everything was. It was her fault he had to dig coal. Her own fault he hit her. If she didn't nag at him he wouldn't have to. Unless he slapped her for the way she was looking at him. He'd start drinking Jim Beam and Diet Coke—ate like a hog and drank diet soda—and she'd see it coming as his disposition turned from stupid to ugly and pretty soon he'd be slapping her, hard. She ran way to Corbin and got a job at the Holiday Inn waiting tables. Bowman found her and brought her back saying he missed her and would try to tolerate her acting up. It was her fault she miscarried after he'd beat her with his belt. Her fault he didn't have a son he could take hunting with him and his creepy brother. She told Bowman there were times he wasn't home Boyd would stop by wanting a drink, and if she gave him one he'd start getting funny, "your own brother." Bowman whipped her for telling him, kept after her with his belt till she fell and hit her head on the stove.

This was the other night. She got up from the floor knowing he would never hit her again.

The next day, Saturday, he walked in smelling of beer and gunfire, like nothing had happened the night before. She had his supper on the table, ham and yams, cream-style corn and leftover okra fixed with tomatoes, because she wanted him sitting down. Once he'd poured his Jim Beam and Diet Coke and took his place at the table, Ava went in the kitchen closet and came out with Bowman's Winchester. He looked up and said with his mouth full of sweet potato what sounded like "The hell you doing with that?"

Ava said, "I'm gonna shoot you, you dummy," and she did, blew him out of the chair.

When the prosecutor asked if she had loaded the rifle before firing it, she paused no more than a second before telling him Bowman always kept it loaded.

Raylan was told Bowman himself couldn't find his house when he was drunk. Go on up along the Clover Fork, or take the Gas Road out to the diversion tunnels and turn right down to a road bears east where a sign says JESUS

SAVES, and it ain't far; start looking for a red Dodge pickup in the yard.

It was one-story with aluminum awnings set high among pines. Raylan got out of the Lincoln Town Car—one Art had taken off some convicted felon and given to Raylan to use—and crossed the yard past the Dodge pickup to the front door.

It opened and he was looking at a woman in a soiled T-shirt worn over an old housedress that hung on her, her dark hair a mess. Ava was forty now, but he knew those eyes staring at him and she knew him, saying, "Oh my God—Raylan," in kind of a prayerful tone.

He stepped into a room with bare walls, worn carpeting, a sofa. "You remember me, huh?"

Ava pushed the door closed. She said, "I never forgot you," and went into his arms as he offered them, a girl he used to like now a woman who'd shot and killed her husband and wanted to be held. He could tell, he could feel her hands holding on to him. She raised her face to say, "I can't believe you're here." He kissed her on the cheek. She kept staring at him with those eyes and he kissed her on the mouth. Now they kept looking at each other until Raylan took off his hat and sailed it over to the sofa. He saw her eyes close, her hands slipping around his neck, and this time it became a serious kiss, their mouths finding the right fit and holding till finally they had to breathe. Now he didn't know what to say. He didn't know why he kissed her other than he wanted to. He could remember wanting to even when she was a teen.

"I had a crush on you," Ava said, "from the time I was twelve years old. I knew you liked me, but you didn't want to show it."

"You were too young."

"I was sixteen when you left. I heard you got married. Are you still?"

Raylan shook his head. "Turned out to be a mistake."

"You want to talk about mistakes . . . I told Bowman I wanted a divorce? He goes, 'You file, you'll never be seen again.' Said I'd disappear from the face of the earth."

"I hear he used to beat you up."

"That last time—I've still got a knot where I fell and hit my head on the stove. You want to feel it?" She was touching her scalp, fingers probing into her wild-looking hair, and her expression changed. She said, "Oh my God, don't look at me," pulling the T-shirt over her head, the hem of the housedress rising to show her legs hurrying away from him. "Close your eyes, I don't want you to see me like this." But then she stopped before going in the bedroom and looked back at him.

"Raylan, the minute you walked in I knew everything would be all right."

The bedroom door closed and he wanted to go knock on it before she started assuming too much. Show her he was a federal marshal and tell her why he was here. But then had to ask himself, Why are you? Art had said she didn't want protection. He'd offer it anyway. No, he was here to get a lead on Boyd. Kissing her had confused his purpose there for a minute.

Raylan walked over to the table where they said Bowman was sitting. He looked in the kitchen at a pile of dishes in the sink—Ava letting her housework go, letting herself go, not knowing what was to become of her. But she had all of a sudden pulled herself together, ashamed of the way she looked, and it sounded like she was expecting him to see her through this. And if she was, what was he supposed to do? For one thing they'd better quit kissing.

It wasn't a minute later the front door banged open and a guy wearing alligator teeth walked in the house.

Gator teeth, spiked hair dyed blond and a tattoo on his chest, part of it showing the way his shirt hung open. He stood there looking Raylan over before saying, "Who in the hell are you, the undertaker?"

Raylan got his hat from the sofa and set it on his head the way he wore it. He said, "I might be undertaking a situation here. Lemme see what you have on your chest," wanting this skinhead with hair to open his shirt.

He did, held it apart to show Raylan his HEIL HITLER tattoo, no weapon stuck in his belt. Raylan decided not to mess with Adolf Hitler, saying now, "You buy that necklace or poach the gator and yank her teeth out?"

It got the skin to squint at him but still wanting to tell, because he said, "I shot her and ate her tail."

Now Raylan squinted to show he was thinking. "That would put you in Florida, around Lake Okeechobee."

It got the skin to tell him, "Belle Glade."

"Is that right?" Raylan reached into his inside pocket for his ID case. "I sent a boy to Starke was from Belle Glade, fella name Dale Crowe Junior." He flipped open the case to show his star. "I'm Raylan Givens, deputy United States marshal." He flipped the case closed. "You mind telling me who you are?"

The skin was staring now like he did mind and had to decide whether or not to tell. Raylan said, "You know your name, don't you?"

"It's Dewey Crowe," the skin said, putting some defiance into the sound of it. "Dale Junior's my kin."

Raylan said, "Man, that's some family you belong to. I know of four Crowes either shot dead or sent to prison. Tell me what you're doing here."

Dewey said, "I come to take Ava someplace," and started toward the bedroom.

Raylan held up his hand and it stopped him.

"Lemme tell you something, Mr. Crowe. You don't walk in a person's house 'less you're invited. What you better do, go on outside and knock on the door. If Ava wants to see you I'll let you in. She doesn't, you can be on your way."

Raylan watched him, curious as to how this boy wearing alligator teeth would take it—big, ugly teeth but no apparent weapon on him.

What he said was, "All right." Keeping it simple to show he was cool. He said, "I'm gonna go out." Paused to set up the rest of it and said, "Then I'm coming back in." He turned and went out the door, leaving it open.

Raylan came over to stand in the doorway. He watched young Mr. Crowe hurrying toward his car standing in the road, an old rusting-out Cadillac, and watched him raise the trunk lid.

Raylan took off his suitcoat and hooked it on the doorknob. He wore a blue shirt with a mostly dark-blue striped tie. He reset his hat on his head. Now his hand went to the grip of the revolver on his right hip, the .45-caliber

Smith & Wesson, but did not clear it from the worn leather holster.

He watched Dewey Crowe bring a pump shotgun out of the trunk and start back this way, all business now, his mind made up, his dumb pride taking him to a place it would be hard to back out of.

Though he hadn't racked the pump to put a shell in the breech.

Still hadn't as he slowed up seeing Raylan in his shirt-sleeves, Dewey Crowe taking careful steps now, holding the shotgun out in front of him.

Raylan said, "Mr. Crowe? Listen, you better hold on there while I tell you something."

It stopped him about fifty feet away, his shoulders hunched.

"I want you to understand," Raylan said, "I don't pull my sidearm 'less I'm gonna shoot to kill. That's its purpose, huh, to kill. So it's how I use it."

Speaking hard words in a quiet tone of voice.

"I want you to think about what I'm saying before you act and it's too late."

"Jesus Christ," Dewey said. "I got a fuckin' scatter gun pointed right at you."

"But can you rack in a load," Raylan said, "before I put a hole through you?"

Raylan stepped out to the yard. He said, "Come on," pushing the barrel of the shotgun aside to take Dewey by the arm and walk him out to the car, a piece of junk but still a Cadillac.

"Where'd you want to take Ava?"

Dewey said, "Man, I don't understand you."

"Boyd want to see her?"

"It's none of your business."

"You know Boyd and I were buddies? We dug coal and drank beer together." Raylan opened the car door. "You see him, tell him I'm in Harlan."

Dewey didn't say anything getting in the car. He had to turn the key a few times before it caught. Raylan reached through the open window and put his hand on his shoulder. "I was you, boy, I'd drop this Nazi bullshit and get back to poaching gators, it's safer."

Dewey looked up at him. As he said, "The next time I see you . . ." only got that far before Raylan took a handful of his spiked hair and brought his head down hard on the windowsill. Raylan hunched over now to look into the face tightened with pain.

"Listen to me. Tell Boyd his old buddy wants to see him, Raylan Givens."

VI.

He went back in the house to find Ava in the kitchen pouring Jim Beam, Ava in a tank top and shorts, her hair wrapped in a towel that was like a white turban around her head. She said, "Who was that?" not sounding too interested. He told her and she said, "Oh, the one with Heil Hitler on his chest, he was one of Bowman's buddies."

"He came to take you someplace."

"Most likely to see Boyd. You want something with yours? I've got Diet Co'Cola, RC Cola, Dr Pepper . . ."

"Just ice, if you have some."

"I ever forget to fill the trays Bowman'd start slapping me. 'What's wrong with you? Don't you know how to keep house?'"

The towel covering her hair made the rest of her seem more exposed, white and kind of puffy, more to her, like she had gained a good twenty pounds since taking off the housedress that hung on her. He saw now it was that wild hair that had made her face appear drawn. He noticed bruises on her pale skin, on her arms and legs, that made her appear soiled, and, oh man, her behind filled out those shorts—Raylan watching her carrying their drinks to the table where she had shot her husband.

"I cleaned it up good. Had to scrub the wall there with Lysol to get, you know, the stains off it. I think Lysol's the best cleaning product you can buy."

Raylan sat down at the table with her. "You haven't seen Boyd, have you? I mean since?"

"No, but he'll be after me, I know. He's *been* after me."

"That's why we want to keep an eye on you," Raylan said. "You know I'm with the Marshals Service."

"I believe was your mother told me, before she passed." Ava lit a cigarette from a pack lying on the table and blew a stream of smoke by him. "I made the mistake of telling Bowman about his brother coming around and he whipped me with his belt. Didn't want to believe it." She drew on the cigarette again. Smoke came out as she said, "Here's a man was so jealous he'd stop by Betty's to check on me."

"Betty's?"

"Hair Salon, where I work, or did. I trained under Betty washing hair, giving perms. I do hair now for special occasions, weddings, graduations I do a bunch of the girls. Yeah, Bowman'd stop by and look in. . . . He'd get on me for the least thing. Like if he found a hair in his baked possum? Or I didn't get out all the scent glands? He'd have a fit, throw his supper at me, the plate, the whole mess."

Raylan listened, sipping his drink, wanting to get back to Boyd.

"I wish I could move, go someplace and open my own hair salon. Where do you live?"

"West Palm Beach."

"Is it nice?"

"Palm trees and traffic, if you're going anywhere."

Ava drew on her cigarette and started to grin. She turned it off exhaling the smoke and said, "I think Bowman's problem, besides being stupid, he wasn't raised properly. He had the worst table manners. Like he'd be sitting here, he'd lean over to one side and get a look like he was concentrating on some deep thought? Furrow his brow and let a fart. It didn't matter he was having his supper. But the worst, oh my Lord, were the beer farts, the next morning when he was hungover? I'd have to leave the house."

Raylan managed to smile, nodding his head.

"That's the way he always was, either drunk or hungover, or gone. Off playing soldier with his brother."

"You have any idea where he is?"

Ava looked at him funny. "I imagine he's in Hell. Where else would he be?"

"I mean Boyd."

"Boyd's on his way there. You gonna arrest him?"

"We have to catch him in the act first. Robbing a bank, blowing up a church . . . making an attempt on your life . . ."

"*Mine?*"

"You said yourself he'll be coming after you."

" 'Cause he likes me. Boyd don't want to shoot me, Raylan, he wants to"—she shrugged in a cute way—"go to bed with me." Ava stubbed out her cigarette, her eyes warm as she looked at him and put her hand on his. "You want me to help you catch him?"

Raylan sipped his drink. "How about if you get him to talk to me?"

"I could do that."

Ava got up and Raylan's gaze followed her into the kitchen. He said, "I hear he has a place up by Sukey Ridge." Then had to wait for Ava to come back to the table with the Jim Beam and a bowl of ice.

"It's his church," Ava said, freshening their drinks. "He's only there when he gets his skinheads together. There's a fun bunch. They sit around drinking beer and listening to black-hater bands, different ones like the Midtown Boot Boys, Dying Breed, all bopping their bald heads. They are *so* creepy."

"Boyd doesn't stay there?"

"Bowman said he has places around nobody knows about, not even all the skins." Ava took a drink and said, " 'Cept I know of one," giving Raylan a sly look with those brown eyes he remembered. "Was Boyd, not Bowman, told me where he stays most of the time."

Raylan took a drink. "You want to tell me where it is?"

Ava said, "What do I get if I do?"

VII.

It was Devil Ellis saw the car headlights out the window, moving up the grade, and told Boyd somebody was coming. Boyd folded the map full of arrows and circles they were looking at and shoved it into the table drawer.

Devil, at the window now, peering out from under his black hat, said, "Who do you know drives a Town Car?"

Walking to the door Boyd said, "Why don't we find out," each being cool in front of the other.

Devil said, "Ain't anyone I've seen before."

Boyd opened the door and watched the man in the cocked Stetson approach out of the dark. Boyd, grinning now because he was glad to see him, said, "It's my old buddy, Raylan Givens."

Raylan had to smile seeing the way Boyd was waiting for him, holding out his arms now, Boyd saying, "God *damn,* look at you, a suit and necktie, all dressed up to look like a lawman." He gave Raylan a hug, patting his back, Raylan letting him for old times' sake. As they stepped apart Boyd looked over at Devil. "Here's how you wear a hat, casual, not down on your goddamn ears."

Raylan looked him over, recalling a Devil Ellis on Art Mullen's skinhead list. This one was giving Raylan a dead-eyed look, showing he wasn't impressed, as Boyd was saying,

"I hear you called on Ava. Boy name Dewey Crowe said he ran you off."

"You believe that?"

"Not if you say it ain't so. Ava's the one told you I was here?"

"I talked her into it. Told her I wouldn't tell anybody."

"How do you know she didn't send you to me?" Boyd winked. "So I could decide what to do with you."

"I'll take care of him," Devil said, wanting in on what was going on.

Raylan didn't bother with him. He said to Boyd, "I doubt she even knows this is the house was foreclosed on. Pretty slick, move back in figuring nobody would look for you here." Raylan saying it as he began to look around at the front room of this farmhouse that was spare of furnishing—a table and a few straight chairs on the linoleum floor—but looked like a gallery with all the white supremacy symbols framed on the wall. There were emblems representing the KKK, Aryan Nations, the Hammerskins, SS thunderbolts, RAHOWA with a death's head that stood for Racial Holy War, swastikas on an Iron Cross, over an eagle, Nazi Party flag with swastika . . . Raylan said, "You all sure like swastikas," and looked over at Boyd. "What's the spiderweb?"

"You get it tattooed on your elbow if you done time or killed some minority, Jew or a jigaboo."

"Boyd, you know any Jews?"

"A few. I also know they run the economy, control the Federal Reserve and the IRS. I recruit skins don't know any more'n you, have to show 'em why we have a moral obligation to get rid of minorities. Read your Bible."

"It's in there?"

"Part of Creation. Back at the beginning of time you got your mud people, referred to as beasts 'cause they don't have souls. Okay, Adam jumped Eve and she begat Abel, the beginning of the white race as God intended. But then Satan in the form of a snake jumped Eve. She begat Cain and things got out of hand. Cain began fucking mud people, the women, and out of these fornications came the Edomites. And you know who the Edomites are?"

"Tell me."

"The Jews."

"You're serious."

"Read your Bible as interpreted by experts."

"Are you born again?"

"Again and again."

"I think you're putting me on," Raylan said, noticing silver chains now hanging from deer antlers, on the wall with photos taken of Boyd in Vietnam. Raylan walked over and Boyd followed him.

"They look like dog turds now, but they's ears I took offa dead gooks I killed. After I got back I use to offer a pair to different women I was seeing."

"No takers, huh?"

"It was like a test. A woman that won't accept a pair and wear 'em proudly ain't the one I'm looking for. We invite these little Nazigirls up to the church? Chelsea girls they're called—shitkickers, hair under their armpits—any one of 'em would wear a pair of the ears, fight over 'em, but they're not my type. I like a woman ain't afraid of nothing but more feminine in her ways, more womanly."

"Like Ava," Raylan said.

"Listen, I called her up—" Boyd stopped and looked over at Devil. "Go on get us a jar and a couple glasses." He raised his voice, "Clean ones," as Devil went out to the kitchen. Boyd turned to Raylan. "He just got his release, so he's looking for action."

"I can tell," Raylan said.

"Was down three years on a marijuana conviction—you know it's grown all around here. Devil couldn't convince the court what he had was for personal use. Four hundred pounds in two refrigerators."

Raylan sensed a connection between Devil and the marijuana church in Cincinnati and said, "We were thinking to sell this house to a black man, see if it might bring you out in the open."

Boyd said, "Your nigger would never've known what hit him."

Devil came with a jar of shine no meaner-looking than water, a few specks of charcoal in it, his fingers in the three glasses he placed on the table.

Boyd shoved one of the glasses back to him. "This is me and Raylan's party. You aren't invited." Devil seemed to want to argue, give a reason to stay. Boyd told him go on, get outta here.

Now he poured their drinks, a few inches of pure corn into each glass. "I don't like him hearing things he's liable to take the wrong way."

Raylan said, "How you feel about Ava?" He took a sip. It was smooth, but caused saliva to rise in his mouth and made him swallow a couple of times.

"I called her up," Boyd said. "I told her the only reason I

didn't take her out and shoot her, I saw she had no choice in what she done. I told her she showed spunk for a woman, not knowing what I'd do about it. I told her another reason was the Bible saying a man should see to the needs of his brother's widow, and that I intended to take care of her."

"Bless your heart," Raylan said.

"Don't get smart with me. I meant it."

"Boyd, you use the Bible to get what you want, same as you use all this white supremacy bullshit to rob banks and raise hell, blow up a church in Cincinnati for the fun of it. See, I'm giving you the benefit you aren't mental. I know you aren't stupid enough to believe that mud people story."

They stood facing each other across the table, the quart mason jar of moonshine between them, Boyd showing his size in a khaki shirt pulled taut across his chest. He appeared calm, his eyes showing interest.

He said, "Raylan, the whole world's gonna become mulatta we don't separate the races quick. I believe that much and it's enough."

Raylan only shrugged. "Then you'll die for it or go to prison."

Boyd looked at him now like he was trying to decide something in his mind.

"You'd shoot me, you get the chance?"

"You make me pull," Raylan said, "I'll put you down."

Devil had the map spread open on the table again, the one with the circles and arrows. He said to Boyd coming back in the house, "You kiss him goodbye?"

Boyd said, "You want your jaw broke?"

"I'm kidding with you," Devil said, waited for Boyd to sit down and hunched over next to him to point out on the map. "Here, we take 421 down across the Virginia line. East on 606 and we come to Nina, not an hour from here."

"How many people?"

"Less'n four hundred. Nearest deputies are at Big Stone Gap. Hit the town, the bank, the stores, bang bang bang, any place there's a cash register. Run up the flag . . . Which one?"

"Rebel battle flag."

"That'd be my choice. We show how a town can be taken over and secured with fifteen militia. How, the time comes, it can be done all over the Jewnited States."

Boyd put his finger on a line Devil had drawn. "I don't see a road here."

"It ain't on the map, Boyd, it's a four-wheeler trail through marijuana country, one of many the growers use. It takes us up to near 38 and we're back home."

Now, as Boyd studied the map, Devil said, "Why'd you let him go? I could've put him away, easy."

Boyd looked up. He said to Devil, "Stick to your recon." Looked at the map again and said, "What I do with Raylan's my business."

Boyd had come outside with him to stand with his hands in his pockets, nodding toward the crest of a slope that had been strip-mined and stood bare against the night sky. He told Raylan they were cutting the tops off of mountains and letting the slag run down to ruin the creeks.

Shaking houses to pieces with their blasting. He reminded
Raylan how their dads had dug coal ten hours a day for eighty
cents. How "me and you" would go into worked-out mines
and chop into the pillars of coal holding up the roof, and run
like hell if she began to cave. Remember? It was called robbing the mine. And how they stood on the picket line the year
they struck Eastover and watched the courts back the company scabs and gun thugs. "Whose side's the govermint always been on, Raylan, us or the people with money? And who
controls the money and wants to mongrelize the world?" That
was his argument, why he felt he could rob banks and kill
anyone wasn't white. There was no talking to him.

Raylan said, "You're gonna stand in a lineup tomorrow,
Harlan County courthouse, nine o'clock."

"What'd I do now?"

"You can show up or we'll come get you."

He made his way down the mountain and through Evarts
past his high school, the Home of the Wildcats, going toward
Harlan till he swung off 38 to follow dirt roads dark as pitch,
no sign other than JESUS SAVES, and would have missed the
house if a light wasn't on—Raylan thinking that if he'd
stayed he'd be living up a hollow in a house like that, a
pickup truck in the yard. . . . But what would he be?

Ava hugged him and gave him a kiss on the
cheek and held on bringing him inside, Ava wearing a loose
sweater now with her shorts, wearing her hair in a soft wave
that came close to one of her brown eyes and a nice scent that
he liked—Raylan sitting with her on the sofa now, their

drinks on the coffee table Bowman must've put his steel-toed workshoes on to get it scarred like it was, Bowman a presence, his wife until a few days ago sitting at the end of the sofa by the lamp shining on her hair.

"Did you see Boyd?"

"I told him he has to come in tomorrow. Boyd blew up a church in Cincinnati and we have a witness who'll take a look at him."

"Well, that was quick. Boy, you work fast," Ava said, raising her eyebrows at him. "And I oughta know."

Right there, Raylan knew he should tell her wait, he wasn't making a move on her. But what he said was, "Boyd might not show up. Even if he does, I'm pretty sure he won't be made, identified."

"So you'll be staying around? Cool."

Ava got up and went to her CD player. She put on Shania Twain and came back singing along, "'Men's shirts, short skirts, oh, *oh*, oh, really go wild, doin' it in style . . .'" The phone rang. Ava turned down the volume on her way to the kitchen. Raylan heard her say, "Who? . . . Oh, yeah, I remember. . . . Listen, hon? I can't talk to you right now, I've got company." Now she was laughing as she hung up the phone. Ava turned the volume back up and joined Shania again singing, "'Oh, *oh*, oh, get in the action, feel the attraction . . .' Fella name Russ. Can you believe he's the second one's called me? I kinda knew 'em from a Fourth of July party we went to. Couple of showoffs. They made a bet, see who could throw down a blue blazer the fastest. You know, you light a shot glass of whiskey? That's a blue blazer. They both threw theirs over their shoulder and banged their shot glasses down at the same time, on the picnic table." Ava shook her head, smiling at the memory. "Cute guys, I'd see them watching me. Now I'm single again they're calling me up. You believe it?"

Ava fell into the sofa to sit low, her head bent against the backrest, her legs apart in the shorts. She turned her head against the cushion to look at Raylan. "Jealous?"

For a moment there, listening to her on the phone, the flirty way she used her voice, he did get a feeling he didn't like. In his head and out again, but it was there.

She said, "Hey, I'm just teasing you. I know you have a life. You must, a cool guy like you? No, I just thought, you're here, why don't we party? I can still do those old Wildcat cheers I know you liked to watch. I still have all the cute moves. Get your motor turned on. You want, Raylan, you can spend the night. How's that sound?"

VIII.

Six A.M. they brought Boyd Crowder down to the courthouse under guard, Art Mullen not trusting the man to walk in on his own. Raylan believed he would. Last night when he called Art, he said the idea of walking in past a gathering of law enforcement people would appeal to Boyd, the man confident he'd walk out again, after.

Raylan made the call from Ava's house after telling her he wouldn't be able to stay the night. She said if he had to get up real early she could set the alarm, it wouldn't bother her none. She said she knew he wanted to. He said well sure he did—

and it was true, he was tempted—but, see, an officer of the law wasn't supposed to go to bed with the defendant in a murder investigation. Ava said oh, she didn't know that. She said well, couldn't they like just fool around?

It was hard to get out of there but he did.

Now he stood in the main corridor of the courthouse. Art Mullen motioned to him and Raylan went over to where Art was standing by an office door, the top part glass. He looked in to see Israel Fandi sitting alone in his dashiki, all different shades of brown with some orange.

"Izzy was telling us," Art said, "how his family from Ethiopia goes back seven hundred years. I said I didn't think Mobile, Alabama, was that old. That's where he's from originally. We turn the lights out in there and line up Boyd out here in the hall. We thought at first with some miners. But you know what Boyd looks like?"

"A cop," Raylan said. "I see his buddy's here, the one they call Devil? And a skinhead from Florida with dyed hair."

"I saw them."

"You let 'em hang around?"

"They raise a ruckus, we can bust 'em."

It wasn't long after, Devil himself strolled up, Dewey Crowe trailing him. Devil said, "What time's the show?" As he looked in the office Art stepped in front of Devil and shoved him aside, Devil saying, "Hey, come on, me and Iz are buds." Art told him to keep away from the door and Devil said, "He never saw Boyd up there in Cincy. Even if he says he did to please you, you know he didn't. But why would he? Iz's going down anyway for the weed."

They brought Boyd along the corridor and stood him in line with three marshals and two ATF agents and turned out the light in the office. It was off a good ten minutes, the lineup standing in place, before it came on again. Raylan noticed Boyd was the only one didn't move or fidget during that time. Now Art came out with the Bureau people who'd been in there with Israel and told Boyd he could go.

Boyd saw Raylan and came over.

"I'm gonna sit down with my lawyer when I leave here. They went through my house saying they had probable cause to look for guns. They tore up my posters and threw 'em in the trash barrel with my gook ears, burned up my private property."

"It wasn't yours," Raylan said. "The house belongs to the Marshals Service. You can understand they don't like all that Nazi shit hanging on their walls."

"It's some govermint can take a man's house from him," Boyd said. He looked up the corridor to where Devil and Dewey Crowe were waiting for him, then back to Raylan.

"Last night this marshal's telling me how one time you gave this fella twenty-four hours to get out of town or you'd shoot him on sight. Is that true?"

"Was a gangster I saw shoot an unarmed man," Raylan said. "I didn't feel he deserved any special favors. I gave him the option and he turned it down."

"Well, all the trouble you're causing me," Boyd said, "I

thought I'd make you the same offer. Get out of Harlan County by tomorrow noon or I'll come looking for you. That sound fair?"

Raylan said to him, "Now you're talking."·

When he told Art Mullen Boyd had set this deadline, Art said, "It's become something personal?" frowning, at first not liking the sound of it.

"That's what it looks like," Raylan said, "since Boyd and I go back, but it isn't. You're the one gave him the idea while you're busting up his house last night."

"Our house," Art said.

They were having their noon dinner of steak and eggs at the Western Sizzlin Steak place out on the 421 bypass.

"I see you and him both cut from the same stock, born a hundred years past your time."

Art had said it once before and it reminded Raylan of a woman named Joyce saying pretty much the same thing but in different words. He was seeing her at the time he shot the gangster in Miami Beach, and Joyce had trouble accepting the fact he had deliberately shot and killed a man. She told him he had an image of himself as a lawman, meaning an Old West lawman but without the big mustache, and he believed it might be true in some deep part of his mind. Another time Joyce said, "The way you put it, you said you called him out. What did you think, you were in a movie?" Her saying it caught him by surprise, because at times he did see it that way, as something he had borrowed from a western movie. He liked westerns a lot.

By the time they were into their flame-kist steak and eggs, both dipping toast into the yolks, Art had come to appreciate Raylan's situation.

"We're like big-game hunters, you know it? Only you're the bait, like a goat tethered to a post. All we have to do is keep you in sight." Art took time to chew up a bite of steak. "What'd he say exactly, *he's* coming for you or *we're* coming?"

"He said *he* was."

"But we don't know if he wants to shoot you or blow you up, do we?"

Raylan, mopping up his plate, didn't comment, letting Art have his fun.

"Or, Boyd might jump the gun," Art said, "do it ahead of time, when you aren't looking. I was you I'd check under the car before you turn the key."

He said later on when they were having their pie, "I knew bringing you here was a good idea."

IX.

Boyd didn't hate Raylan any more'n he'd hated those dead gooks without ears. Taking Raylan out was like a military objective, better to look at with a clear head than get emotional about it. Up at Sukey Ridge he told the skinheads gathered for the raid into Virginia he was putting it on hold, there was a matter he had to settle first. The skins gave him their shrugs and popped open beers.

He had already put the two locals, the Pork brothers, up on that hill that was behind the Mount-Aire Motel, where Raylan and the rest of the feds were staying. The brothers had

Russian binoculars, deer rifles, an AK-47 and a cell phone and were told to stay in the trees and watch for Raylan Givens. Call and report whenever his Town Car came or went, a big shiny Lincoln losing its shine. One of the Pork brothers said, "What if we get a clear shot at him?"

Boyd wasn't sure they could hit the motel from beyond two hundred yards, but it gave him an idea. How to set Raylan up and get him off by himself. He told the Pork brothers to sit tight, he'd let them know.

He told Devil Ellis and the skin who wore the alligator teeth, Dewey, he was thinking of taking his shot that night. It was Devil said, "I thought you were giving him twenty-four hours."

Boyd said what that actually meant was the next time you saw the person, not the next day to the hour. Hell, the guy would be dug in waiting on you. He said, "I know Raylan ain't leaving, so I may as well hit him when it suits me." He told them he had considered waiting across the road from the motel with an RPG and when the Town Car pulled in blow it to hell. "But there's no cover over there to speak of, the mall close by," Boyd said, "and I'd as soon plug him face-to-face anyway."

Both Devil and Dewey said they wanted to be there when he did, and Boyd surprised them saying they would, as they were gonna be his backup. They acted tickled to death till he said, "You know Raylan will have his own people," and could tell they hadn't thought of that. But then he said, "How'd we keep the law busy when we robbed those banks?" It got their heads nodding, both of 'em grinning, showing they still wanted to be along. "I've thought of a way to keep the feds out of the picture," Boyd said, "if we can get the timing down. The idea, separate Mr. Givens from his pack of suits and get him off by hisself."

Oh boy, they liked the sound of that, asking how they'd do it, blow up a car? Boyd said, "I got another plan. What I want you fellas to do is locate Raylan and let me know where he's at, from now on."

Late afternoon, Raylan came out of Art Mullen's office in the courthouse to see Ava coming along the corridor in a beige outfit, skirt and sweater, pearls, Ava getting better-looking by the day, her expression becoming a big smile as she came up to him.

"My lawyer's still talking to the prosecutor, but it's looking good. Come on with me while I have a smoke."

She took him outside, saw the benches on Central Street occupied—"Geezers're always sitting there," Ava said—and they went over to the bench in front of the Coal Miners Memorial: six columns of dead miners close to ten feet high, Raylan's dad's name among them. He found it as Ava, smoking her cigarette, told him she was pretty sure she'd get off with no more'n probation. "I plead to some kind of manslaughter and I won't have to go to prison. Hey, why don't you come by for supper? I'll fix you something nice."

Raylan said, "Baked possum?"

"I only cooked that for Bowman. I got mad at him one time and put roach powder in it? He goes, 'Honey, this is the best possum I ever et.' Didn't even get sick. I'll pick up a couple of nice fryers and fix you some hot biscuits and gravy." She grinned at him. "Look at you licking your lips."

Raylan said all his life fried chicken was his favorite, but he had to hang around, didn't know when he'd be off.

Ava said, "I'm fixing it anyway." She looked him in the eye saying, "You're a big boy, Raylan. You want to come, there's nothing on earth gonna stop you."

Devil had his hair cut and beard trimmed at the Cumberland Barber Shop, across the side street from the courthouse. He put on his hat and got in Dewey's junk Cadillac, parked in front of the shop. Dewey said, "You missed it. He come out with Ava, they talked and he went back in again. You said you thought that red Dodge over on Central was Bowman's? It was. Ava got in it and drove away."

Devil said, "Wasn't for Boyd I'd have me some of Ava."

Dewey said, "Wasn't for Boyd me and you could have us the marshal. Say we took him out, what would Boyd do, kick and scream? He does that anyways."

Devil said, "You got the nerve to shoot a marshal?"

Dewey said, "I got the nerve and a reason to."

They were silent, thinking about it, till Devil said, "That barber didn't say one goddamn word to me the whole time he's cutting my hair."

Ten of six they watched Raylan come out of the courthouse with four other suits and go to their cars parked on Central.

Dewey said, "We get out on the highway—you're driving

'cause it's my idea—I reach in back for the twelve-gauge and blow him away. What's wrong with that?"

Devil said there wasn't nothing wrong with it.

Except once they got to 421 two other marshal cars were on Raylan's tail all the way to the Mount-Aire Motel. Devil called Boyd to tell him Raylan was back in his room.

"Roger that," Boyd said, and told Devil, "Okay, he should be leaving again pretty soon. I got a way to bring him to me I think'll work. He leaves, you stay on him."

Devil's voice said, "Where you at?" sounding surprised.

"Down the road from Ava's. You stay on him, hear?"

Boyd sat in his Jeep Cherokee by the JESUS SAVES sign, the road here like a tunnel through the trees, dark as night. He called the Pork brothers on the hill behind the motel and told them to get ready. "You saw him come back? . . . Okay, you see his car pull out again, you let it go. Understand? But then any other cars pull out to follow him? You open up on 'em. Pour it on, as many rounds as you can squeeze off."

The Pork brother on the phone said it was near dark, how would they see the cars? Boyd said, "Jesus Christ, they put their lights on, don't they? Aim back of the headlights."

Boyd believed the suits would spot 'em and swarm up there with sheriff's deputies and state police and shoot those two fat boys down, but didn't see losing them would handicap him any. It was the reason the Pork brothers were up there.

He drove through the tunnel of trees to a semidry creekbed

he turned into and stopped about fifty yards in to leave the Jeep. It was a place he'd used to slip up on the house, make sure Bowman wasn't home. It was close by. Boyd moved through the pines toward a light shining in the front room, meaning she was home. He rapped on the door. It opened, and he saw right away Ava was expecting company.

X.

She had on her party dress, the shiny green low-cut one with the straight skirt she'd worn to Bowman's funeral. Seeing Boyd instead of Raylan gave her a start and all she could say was, "Well, hi," disappointed. There was nothing to hide, so she told Boyd she'd invited Raylan for a home-cooked supper but didn't know if he'd make it or not.

Boyd came in sniffing, saying, "Mmmmmm, fried chicken." Saying, "Why don't you call Raylan and remind him? Go on, he's at the Mount-Aire." And gave her the phone number.

Well, then she became suspicious. Why would Boyd know that? "You've talked to him?"

"Honey, me and Raylan are old buddies. I thought you knew that?"

She hesitated because it sounded fishy.

"Go on, give him a call. But don't say I'm here."

"Why not?"

"I'm not staying," Boyd said, "so why mention it. I can see you want to flirt with him some."

"We was neighbors," Ava said, "that's all."

"I know, and you want to talk about old times and so on. Go on, call him."

Raylan picked up the phone to hear Ava asking if he could smell the chicken frying. "It'll be done by the time you get here." Raylan, sitting on the side of his bed, took a few moments before telling Ava he was on his way.

He went next door to Art Mullen's room to let him know he was going. Art said, "You don't see it as Boyd using her?"

"I would," Raylan said, "except she asked me this afternoon, at the courthouse."

"She could've been setting you up then," Art said. "I think we'll tag along."

Raylan didn't argue. He drew Art a quick map showing how to get to Ava's and left.

Dewey saw headlights pop on, the Town Car out from the motel, and hit Devil's arm, Devil still behind the wheel, Devil adjusting his hat as he turned the key and the starter groaned without catching. "You're gonna flood it," Dewey said. "Pump the gas pedal twice and try it." It worked, the engine roaring to life, and they took off east after the Town Car, Dewey saying, "Now catch the son of a bitch, will you?" He reached over his seat for the shotgun and saw out the rear window another car pulling away from the motel and heard gunfire, an automatic weapon, and saw sparks jumping off the road behind the car, the car swerving, U-turning back to the motel with its headlights off. Now a rifle was firing along with the bursts from the AK, Devil hunched over the wheel saying, "Jesus Christ," and Dewey saying, "It's the fat boys, up on the yan side of the mo-tel, holding 'em down. Come on, man, put your foot in it."

Raylan saw the headlights trailing him. He came to the diversion tunnels, drilled through the mountain to run off floodwater, made his turn south and slowed down to watch. Now the headlights behind him made the turn and Raylan took off, holding the car in deep ruts all the way to the JESUS SAVES sign, where he made his turn into the deep tunnel of trees, the dirt road here not much wider than the car.

They saw they weren't going to catch him, no way. They'd drive on up to Ava's and do what Boyd said, back him while he made his play. Dewey said he hoped they'd get there before Boyd shot him. Man, that was something he wanted to see.

Devil, his eyes stuck on the narrow road, said, "Christ Almighty . . ." The Cadillac headlights coming onto the rear end of the Town Car sitting in the road, its lights off, the Cadillac creeping now, Devil taking his time, saying, "The hell's he doing?" as they came to a stop about twenty feet short of that black rear deck shining in their headlights.

Dewey said, "He must be sneaking up on the house."

Devil looked toward Dewey and said, "No, he ain't," because there was Raylan standing at Dewey's side of the car, resting his hands now on the sill right next to Dewey. They *had* to say something to him, Devil wanting to know what the hell he thought he was doing, Dewey asking why he was blocking the fuckin' road.

Raylan didn't say a word, not till he opened the door and slipped into the back, picked up the shotgun and rested the barrel on the front seat, between the cowboy hat and the gator killer's dyed hair.

He said, "Tell me what's going on."

Silence, neither one of them saying a word.

Raylan racked the shotgun and saw them jump.

"I didn't hear you."

"There ain't nothing going on," Devil said. "We's out riding around."

Raylan squeezed the trigger, putting a big hole in the windshield with the explosion, and the two skins clamped their hands over their ears, turning their heads back and forth.

Raylan racked the pump again and Devil said, "Boyd wants to talk to you is all."

"He told me he's gonna shoot me."

Dewey turned his head to say, "Then what're you asking us for, asshole?" and Raylan laid the shotgun barrel across his face, a quick hard stroke that drew blood from his nose.

Raylan said, "An outlaw's life's hard, ain't it?"

He fished handcuffs from his belt and gave them to Devil on the muzzle end of the shotgun, telling him to cuff his right hand, put it through the steering wheel and cuff the gator killer. "Now hand me your pistols."

"We don't have none," Devil said.

"All right," Raylan said, "but if you're telling me a story

I'm gonna break your nose like I broke Mr. Crowe's. That okay with you?"

It got him a couple of Beretta nines.

"And the car keys."

Raylan got out, went around to the back of the Cadillac and called Art Mullen's pager. While he waited he opened the trunk to see a couple of Kalashnikovs inside, threw the pistols in there and closed the trunk. He looked in the car again, on Devil's side this time, and said, "You fellas wait here, okay?"

His cell phone buzzed as he was moving through the trees toward Ava's house. It was Art Mullen, Art telling how they were bushwhacked by a couple of baldheaded kids with a machine gun. "Fired at the cars but didn't hit either one, so nobody's hurt. We went up after 'em with sheriff's people and the kids threw down their weapons. I'm still up on the hill, behind the motel. Where're you?"

Raylan told him and Art said, "Wait for us, we won't be long."

"I'll go slow," Raylan said. "If I see he's laying for me I'll hang back. But let's find out where he is."

He was still holding the shotgun, pointed down at his side, going up to the door. Ava opened it and stood there. He didn't care too much for the green dress or the way she was looking at him. He said, "Don't feel you have to say anything."

But she did. "I swear to God, Raylan, I didn't know he was coming."

He believed her and told her so in a nice tone of voice. He

wanted to tell her it was a pretty dress, but couldn't. He waited and now Ava motioned with her head as she moved aside. Raylan stepped through the doorway to see Boyd at the table that was laid out with a platter of chicken, bowls of mashed potatoes, peas and carrots, a plate of biscuits and a gravy boat. It looked like Boyd had already started, white gravy covering everything on his plate, a pistol lying next to it. Boyd picked it up.

Raylan saw it was an old Army Colt .45 as it came to point at the shotgun he was holding at his side. Boyd said, "No shotguns allowed." He told Ava to take it and throw it outside, then motioned with the .45 for Raylan to come over to the table.

"Sit at that end and help yourself. The gravy ain't bad, but not as good as your mama's. It never is, huh?"

Raylan took his place and Boyd said, "When you shot the guy, that wop? You were sitting at a table like this?"

"We were a little closer."

"There was food on the table?"

"No, but it was set, glasses, dishes."

"Have something."

Raylan picked up a drumstick and held it in his left hand to take a bite.

"You had your gun—what was it?"

"That time? A Beretta nine, same as your two morons were packing."

Boyd said, "I believe I heard one shot."

"That's all it took. They're waiting in the car."

"Which one'd you shoot?"

"Neither, but they're out of business."

Boyd said, "You're sitting at the table," getting back to it. "Where was your gun—where mine is?"

"It was holstered."

"Bullshit."

"It was holstered."

"Where was his?"

"In a beach bag, between his knees."

"He's going swimmin' and stops off?"

Raylan didn't answer that one.

"What'd he have in the bag—what kind of piece?"

"I don't recall."

"How'd you know when to pull?"

"Somebody yelled he had a gun."

Boyd paused, staring the length of the table, about eight feet, at Raylan. "You give him twenty-four hours—the time was up when you shot him?"

"Pretty close. I'd remind him how much time he had left. Ten minutes, two minutes . . . I believe we got down to around twenty seconds . . ."

"You're looking at your watch?"

"Estimating the time."

"How much you think you got left now?"

"I thought till noon tomorrow."

"I'm saying it's right now, less you want to eat first."

"You can call it off," Raylan said. "I don't mind."

Boyd shook his head. "If you're gonna keep after me, we may as well get 'er done."

"Your forty-five's on the table but I have to pull," Raylan said. "Is that how we do it?"

"Well, shit yeah, it's my call. What're you packing?"

"You'll pay to find that out," Raylan said.

"Ice water in your veins, huh? You want a shot of Jim Beam to go with it?" Boyd looked away from the table saying, "Ava, get Raylan—" and stopped.

Ava had the shotgun pointed at him, stock under her arm, finger on the trigger.

She said to Boyd, "You want to hear my story, how I shot Bowman? He never sat on the end, he liked the long side of the table so he could spread out, rest his elbows when he was eating fried chicken or corn'n the cob. You want to know what Bowman said when he looked up like you did and saw me with his deer rifle?"

Boyd said, "Honey, you only shoot people when they're having their supper?" He looked at Raylan for appreciation and got a deadpan stare.

"Bowman's mouth was full of sweet potato," Ava said. "I watched him shovel it in as I come out from the kitchen with the rifle. He said, 'The hell you doing with that?' "

Boyd said, "Honey, put it down, would you, please?" He picked up a paper napkin and began wiping his hands.

Raylan took one and stuck it in his shirt collar. He kept his hand there, the right one, smoothing the napkin, the hand that would slide down the lapel of his suitcoat, sweep it open and in the same motion cover the walnut grip of his gun and pull it high to clear the six-and-a-half-inch barrel. He saw himself doing it.

And saw himself in the Cadillac with the shotgun blowing a hole in the windshield and tried to remember if he'd racked the pump after, because he sure didn't hear Ava rack it.

She was telling Boyd, "And you know what I said to Bowman? I said, 'I'm gonna shoot you, you dummy.' "

Raylan saw her jerk the shotgun to her cheek.

Saw Boyd bringing up the Colt, putting it on her.

And had no choice. Raylan pulled and shot Boyd dead center, the force of it punching him out of his chair as Ava in her party dress fired the shotgun and a 12-gauge pattern ripped into the bare wall.

It told Raylan he must've racked it.

Ava said, "I missed, huh?"

She watched Raylan get up, the gun still in his hand, walk around to Boyd and stoop down over him.

"Is he dead?"

Raylan didn't answer. She saw him go to his knees then to bend close to Boyd's face. She believed Raylan said something, a word or two, but wasn't sure.

"Isn't he dead?"

Raylan got to his feet saying, "He is now."

Art Mullen arrived wanting to know how the rear end of the Town Car got fragged, but saved asking when he saw Boyd on the floor. Raylan stood by, relating the scene step by step as Art rolled Boyd over to look at the exit wound. He said there wasn't any doubt in his mind, a single shot from a high-caliber weapon had done the job. Art looked up at Raylan.

"He have any last words?"

"He said I'd killed him." Raylan paused. "I told him I was sorry, but he had called it."

Art was frowning now. "You're sorry you killed him?"

"I thought I explained it to you," Raylan said in his quiet voice. "Boyd and I dug coal together."

KAREN MAKES OUT

They danced until Karen said she had to be up early tomorrow. No argument, he walked with her through the crowd outside Monaco, then along Ocean Drive in the dark to her car. He said, "Lady, you wore me out." He was in his forties, weathered but young-acting, natural, didn't come on with any singles-bar bullshit buying her a drink, or comment when she said thank you, she'd have Jim Beam on the rocks. They had cooled off by the time they reached her Honda and he took her hand and gave her a peck on the cheek saying he hoped to see her again. In no hurry to make something happen. That was fine with Karen. He said, "Ciao," and walked off.

Two nights later they left Monaco, came out of that pounding sound to a sidewalk café and drinks, and he became Carl Tillman, skipper of a charter deep-sea-fishing boat out of American Marina, Bahia Mar. He was single, married seven years and divorced, no children; he lived in a ground-floor two-bedroom apartment in North

Miami—one of the bedrooms full of fishing gear he didn't know where else to store. Carl said his boat was out of the water, getting ready to move it to Haulover Dock, closer to where he lived.

Karen liked his weathered, kind of shaggy look, the crow's-feet when he smiled. She liked his soft brown eyes that looked right at her as he talked about making his living on the ocean, about hurricanes, the trendy scene here on South Beach, movies. He went to the movies every week and told Karen—raising his eyebrows in a vague, kind of stoned way—his favorite actor was Jack Nicholson. Karen asked him if that was his Nicholson impression or was he doing Christian Slater doing Nicholson? He told her she had a keen eye; but couldn't understand why she thought Dennis Quaid was a hunk. That was okay.

He said, "You're a social worker."

Karen said, "A *social* worker—"

"A teacher."

"What kind of teacher?"

"You teach psychology. College level."

She shook her head.

"English lit."

"I'm not a teacher."

"Then why'd you ask what kind I thought you were?"

She said, "You want me to tell you what I do?"

"You're a lawyer. Wait. The Honda—you're a public defender." Karen shook her head and he said, "Don't tell me, I want to guess, even if it takes a while." He said, "If that's okay with you."

Fine. Some guys, she'd tell them what she did and they

were turned off by it. Or they'd act surprised and then self-conscious and start asking stupid questions. "But how can a girl do that?" Assholes.

That night in the bathroom brushing her teeth Karen stared at her reflection. She liked to look at herself in mirrors: touch her short blond hair, check out her fanny in profile, long legs in a straight skirt above her knees, Karen still a size six approaching thirty. She didn't think she looked like a social worker or a schoolteacher, even college level. A lawyer maybe, but not a public defender. Karen was low-key high style. She could wear her favorite Calvin Klein suit, the black one her dad had given her for Christmas, her SIG Sauer .380 for evening wear snug against the small of her back, and no one would think for a moment she was packing.

Her new boyfriend called and stopped by her house in Coral Gables Friday evening in a white BMW convertible. They went to a movie and had supper and when he brought her home they kissed in the doorway, arms slipping around each other, holding, Karen thanking God he was a good kisser, comfortable with him, but not quite ready to take her clothes off. When she turned to the door he said, "I can wait. You think it'll be long?"

Karen said, "What're you doing Sunday?"

They kissed the moment he walked in and made love in the afternoon, sunlight flat on the window shades, the bed stripped down to a fresh white sheet. They made love in a hurry because they couldn't wait, had at each other and lay perspiring after. When they made love again, Karen holding his lean body between her legs and not wanting to let go, it lasted and lasted and got them smiling at each other, saying things like "Wow" and "Oh, my God," it was so good, serious business but really fun. They went out for a while, came back to her yellow stucco bungalow in Coral Gables and made love on the living-room floor.

Carl said, "We could try it again in the morning."

"I have to be dressed and out of here by six."

"You're a flight attendant."

She said, "Keep guessing."

   Monday morning Karen Sisco was outside the federal courthouse in Miami with a pump-action shotgun on her hip. Karen's right hand gripped the neck of the stock, the barrel extending above her head. Several more U.S. deputy marshals were out here with her; while inside, three Colombian nationals were being charged in District Court with the possession of cocaine in excess of five hundred kilograms. One of the marshals said he hoped the scudders liked Atlanta, as they'd be doing thirty to life there pretty soon. He said, "Hey, Karen, you want to go with me, drop 'em off? I know a nice ho-tel we could stay at."

She looked over at the good-ole-boy marshals grinning, shuffling their feet, waiting for her reply. Karen said, "Gary, I'd go with you in a minute if it wasn't a mortal sin." They liked that. It was funny, she'd been standing here thinking she'd gone to bed with four different boyfriends in her life: an Eric at Florida Atlantic, a Bill right after she graduated, then a Greg, three years of going to bed with Greg, and now Carl. Only four in her whole life, but two more than the national average for women in the U.S. according to *Time* magazine, their report of a recent sex survey. The average woman had two partners in her lifetime, the average man six. Karen had thought everybody was getting laid with a lot more different ones than that.

She saw her boss now, Milt Dancey, an old-time marshal in charge of court support, come out of the building to stand looking around, a pack of cigarettes in his hand. Milt looked this way and gave Karen a nod, but paused to light a cigarette before coming over. A guy from the Miami FBI office was with him.

Milt said, "Karen, you know Daniel Burdon?"

Not Dan, not Danny, Daniel. Karen knew him, one of the younger black guys over there, tall and good-looking, confident, known to brag about how many women he'd had of all kinds and color. He'd flashed his smile at Karen one time, hitting on her. Karen turned him down saying, "You have two reasons you want to go out with me." Daniel, smiling, said he knew of one reason, what was the other one? Karen said, "So you can tell your buddies you banged a marshal." Daniel said, "Yeah, but you could use it, too, girl. Brag on getting *me* in the sack." See? That's the kind of guy he was.

Milt said, "He wants to ask you about a Carl Tillman."

No flashing smile this time, Daniel Burdon had on a serious, sort of innocent expression, saying to her, "You know the man, Karen? Guy in his forties, sandy hair, goes about five-ten, one-sixty?"

Karen said, "What's this, a test? Do I *know* him?"

Milt reached for her shotgun. "Here, Karen, lemme take that while you're talking."

She turned a shoulder saying, "It's okay, I'm not gonna

shoot him," her fist tight on the neck of the 12-gauge. She said to Daniel, "You have Carl under surveillance?"

"Since last Monday."

"You've seen us together—so what's this do-I-know-him shit? You playing a game with me?"

"What I meant to ask, Karen, was how long have you known him?"

"We met last week, Tuesday."

"And you saw him Thursday, Friday, spent Sunday with him, went to the beach, came back to your place . . . What's he think about you being with the Marshals Service?"

"I haven't told him."

"How come?"

"He wants to guess what I do."

"Still working on it, huh? What you think, he a nice guy? Has a sporty car, has money, huh? He a pretty big spender?"

"Look," Karen said, "why don't you quit dickin' around and tell me what this is about, okay?"

"See, Karen, the situation's so unusual," Daniel said, still with the innocent expression, "I don't know how to put it, you know, delicately. Find out a U.S. marshal's fucking a bank robber."

Milt Dancey thought Karen was going to swing at Daniel with the shotgun. He took it from her this time and told the Bureau man to behave himself, watch his mouth if he wanted cooperation here. Stick to the facts. This Carl Tillman was a *suspect* in a bank robbery, a possible suspect in a half-dozen more, all the robberies, judging from the bank videos, committed by the same guy. The FBI referred to him as "Slick," having nicknames for all their perps. They had prints off a teller's counter might be the guy's, but no match in their files and not enough evidence on Carl Edward Tillman—the name on his driver's license and car registration—to bring him in. He appeared to be most recently cherry, just getting into a career of crime. His motivation, pissed off at banks because Florida Southern foreclosed on his note and sold his forty-eight-foot Hatteras for nonpayment.

It stopped Karen for a moment. He might've lied about his boat, telling her he was moving it to Haulover; but that didn't make him a bank robber. She said, "What've you got, a video picture, a teller identified him?"

Daniel said, "Since you mentioned it," taking a Bureau wanted flyer from his inside coat pocket, the sheet folded once down the middle. He opened it and Karen was looking at four photos taken from bank video cameras of robberies in progress, the bandits framed in teller windows, three black guys, one white.

Karen said, "Which one?" and Daniel gave her a look before pointing to the white guy: a man with slicked-back hair, an earring, a full mustache, and dark sunglasses. She said, "That's not Carl Tillman," and felt instant relief. There was no resemblance.

"Look at it good."

"What can I tell you? It's not him."

"Look at the nose."

"You serious?"

"That's your friend Carl's nose."

It was. Carl's slender, rather elegant nose. Or like his.

Karen said, "You're going with a nose ID, that's all you've got?"

"A witness," Daniel said, "believes she saw this man—right after what would be the first robbery he pulled—run from the bank to a strip mall up the street and drive off in a white BMW convertible. The witness got a partial on the license number and that brought us to your friend Carl."

Karen said, "You ran his name and date of birth . . ."

"Looked him up in NCIC, FCIC, and Warrant Information, drew a blank. That's why I think he's just getting his feet wet. Managed to pull off a few, two three grand each, and found himself a new profession."

"What do you want me to do," Karen said, "get his prints on a beer can?"

Daniel raised his eyebrows. "That would be a start. Might even be all we need. What I'd like you to do, Karen, is snuggle up to the man and find out his secrets. You know what I'm saying—intimate things, like did he ever use another name . . ."

"Be your snitch," Karen said, knowing it was a mistake as soon as the words were out of her mouth.

It got Daniel's eyebrows raised again. He said, "That what it sounds like to you? I thought you were a federal agent, Karen. Maybe you're too close to him—is that it? Don't want the man to think ill of you?"

Milt said, "That's enough of that shit," standing up for Karen as he would for any of his people, not because she was a woman; he had learned not to open doors for her. The only time she wanted to be first through the door was on a fugitive warrant, this girl who scored higher with a handgun, more times than not, than any other marshal in the Southern District of Florida.

Daniel was saying, "Man, I need to use her. Is she on our side or not?"

Milt handed Karen her shotgun. "Here, you want to shoot him, go ahead."

"Look," Daniel said, "Karen can get me a close read on the man, where he's lived before, if he ever went by other names, if he has any identifying marks on his body, scars, maybe a gunshot wound, tattoos, things only lovely Karen would see when the man has his clothes off."

Karen took a moment. She said, "There is one thing I noticed."

"Yeah? What's that?"

"He's got the letters f-u-o-n tattooed on his penis."

Daniel frowned at her. "Foo-on?"

"That's when it's, you might say, limp. When he has a hard-on it says Fuck the Federal Bureau of Investigation."

Daniel Burdon grinned at Karen. He said, "Girl, you and I have to get together. I mean it."

Karen could handle "girl." Go either way. Girl, looking at herself in a mirror applying blush-on. Woman, well, that's what she was. Though until just a few years ago she only thought of women old enough to be her mother as women. Women getting together to form organizations of women, saying, Look, we're different from men. Isolating themselves in these groups instead of mixing it up with men and beating them at their own men's games. Men in general

were stronger physically than women. Some men were
stronger than other men, and Karen was stronger than some
too; so what did that prove? If she had to put a man on the
ground, no matter how big or strong he was, she'd do it. One
way or another. Up front, in his face. What she couldn't see
herself playing was this sneaky role. Trying to get the stuff on
Carl, a guy she liked, a lot, would think of with tender feelings and miss him during the day and want to be with him.
Shit. . . . Okay, she'd play the game, but not undercover.
She'd first let him know she was a federal officer and see what
he thought about it.

Could Carl be a bank robber?

She'd reserve judgment. Assume almost anyone could at
one time or another and go from there.

What Karen did, she came home and put a pot
roast in the oven and left her bag on the kitchen table, open,
the grip of a Beretta nine sticking out in plain sight.

Carl arrived, they kissed in the living room, Karen feeling
it but barely looking at him. When he smelled the pot roast
cooking, Karen said, "Come on, you can make the drinks
while I put the potatoes on." In the kitchen, then, she stood
with the refrigerator door open, her back to Carl, giving him
time to notice the pistol. Finally he said, "Jesus, you're a cop."

She had rehearsed this moment. The idea: turn saying,
"You guessed," sounding surprised; then look at the pistol
and say something like "Nuts, I gave it away." But she didn't.
He said, "Jesus, you're a cop," and she turned from the refrigerator with an ice tray and said, "Federal. I'm a U.S. marshal."

"I would never've guessed," Carl said, "not in a million years."

Thinking about it before, she didn't know if he'd wig out or what. She looked at him now, and he seemed to be taking it okay, smiling a little.

He said, "But why?"

"Why what?"

"Are you a marshal?"

"Well, first of all, my dad has a company, Marshall Sisco Investigations. . . ."

"You mean because of his name, Marshall?"

"What I am—they're not spelled the same. No, but as soon as I learned to drive I started doing surveillance jobs for him. Like following some guy who was trying to screw his insurance company, a phony claim. I got the idea of going into law enforcement. So after a couple of years at Miami I transferred to Florida Atlantic and got in their Criminal Justice program."

"I mean why not FBI, if you're gonna do it, or DEA?"

"Well, for one thing, I liked to smoke grass when I was younger, so DEA didn't appeal to me at all. Secret Service guys I met were so fucking secretive, you ask them a question, they'd go, 'You'll have to check with Washington on that.' See, different federal agents would come to school to give talks. I got to know a couple of marshals—we'd go out after, have a few beers, and I liked them. They're nice guys, condescending at first, naturally; but after a few years they got over it."

Carl was making drinks now, Early Times for Karen, Dewar's in his glass, both with a splash. Standing at the sink, letting the faucet run, he said, "What do you do?"

"I'm on court security this week. My regular assignment is warrants. We go after fugitives, most of them parole violators."

Carl handed her a drink. "Murderers?"

"If they were involved in a federal crime when they did it. Usually drugs."

"Bank robbery, that's federal, isn't it?"

"Yeah, some guys come out of corrections and go right back to work."

"You catch many?"

"Bank robbers?" Karen said. "Nine out of ten," looking right at him.

Carl raised his glass. "Cheers."

While they were having dinner at the kitchen table he said, "You're quiet this evening."

"I'm tired, I was on my feet all day, with a shotgun."

"I can't picture that," Carl said. "You don't look like a U.S. marshal, or any kind of cop."

"What do I look like?"

"A knockout. You're the best-looking girl I've ever been this close to. I got a pretty close look at Mary Elizabeth Mastrantonio, when they were here shooting *Scarface*? But you're a lot better looking. I like your freckles."

"I used to be loaded with them."

"You have some gravy on your chin. Right here."

Karen touched it with her napkin. She said, "I'd like to see your boat."

He was chewing pot roast and had to wait before saying, "I told you it was out of the water?"

"Yeah?"

"I don't have the boat anymore. It was repossessed when I fell behind in my payments."

"The bank sold it?"

"Yeah, Florida Southern. I didn't want to tell you when we first met. Get off to a shaky start."

"But now that you can tell me I've got gravy on my chin . . ."

"I didn't want you to think I was some kind of loser."

"What've you been doing since?"

"Working as a mate, up at Haulover."

"You still have your place, your apartment?"

"Yeah, I get paid, I can swing that, no problem."

"I have a friend in the marshals lives in North Miami, on Alamanda off a Hundred and Twenty-fifth."

Carl nodded. "That's not far from me."

"You want to go out after?"

"I thought you were tired."

"I am."

"Then why don't we stay home?" Carl smiled. "What do you think?"

"Fine."

They made love in the dark. He wanted to turn the lamp on, but Karen said no, leave it off.

Geraldine Regal, the first teller at Sun Federal on Kendall Drive, watched a man with slicked-back hair and sunglasses fishing in his inside coat pocket as he approached her window. It was nine-forty, Tuesday morning. At first she thought the guy was Latin. Kind of cool, except that up close his hair looked shellacked, almost metallic. She wanted to ask him if it hurt. He brought papers, deposit slips, and a blank check from the pocket saying, "I'm gonna make this out for four thousand." Began filling out the check and said, "You hear about the woman trapeze artist, her husband's divorcing her?"

Geraldine said she didn't think so, smiling, because it was a little weird, a customer she'd never seen before telling her a joke.

"They're in court. The husband's lawyer asks her, 'Isn't it true that on Monday, March the 5th, hanging from the trapeze upside down, without a net, you had sex with the ringmaster, the lion tamer, two clowns, and a dwarf?' "

Geraldine waited. The man paused, head down as he finished making out the check. Now he looked up.

"The woman trapeze artist thinks for a minute and says, 'What was that date again?' "

Geraldine was laughing as he handed her the check, smiling as she saw it was a note written on a blank check, neatly printed in block letters, that said:

> THIS IS NO JOKE
> IT'S A STICKUP!
> I WANT $4000 NOW!

Geraldine stopped smiling. The guy with the metallic hair was telling her he wanted it in hundreds, fifties, and twenties, loose, no bank straps or rubber bands, no bait money, no dye packs, no bills off the bottom of the drawer, and he wanted his note back. Now.

"The teller didn't have four grand in her drawer," Daniel Burdon said, "so the guy settled for twenty-eight hundred and was out of there. Slick changing his style—we *know* it's the same guy, with the shiny hair? Only now he's the Joker. The trouble is, see, I ain't Batman."

Daniel and Karen Sisco were in the hallway outside the central courtroom on the second floor, Daniel resting his long frame against the railing, where you could look below at the atrium with its fountain and potted palms.

"No witness to see him hop in his BMW this time. The man coming to realize that was dumb, using his own car."

Karen said, "Or it's not Carl Tillman."

"You see him last night?"

"He came over."

"Yeah, how was it?"

Karen looked up at Daniel's deadpan expression. "I told him I was a federal agent and he didn't freak."

"So he's cool, huh?"

"He's a nice guy."

"Cordial. Tells jokes robbing banks. I talked to the people at Florida Southern, where he had his boat loan? Found out he was seeing one of the tellers. Not at the main office, one of their branches, girl named Kathy Lopez. Big brown eyes, cute as a puppy, just started working there. She's out with

Tillman she tells him about her job, what she does, how she's counting money all day. I asked was Tillman interested, want to know anything in particular? Oh, yeah, he wanted to know what she was supposed to do if the bank ever got robbed. So she tells him about dye packs, how they work, how she gets a two-hundred-dollar bonus if she's ever robbed and can slip one in with the loot. The next time he's in, cute little Kathy Lopez shows him one, explains how you walk out the door with a pack of fake twenties? A half minute later the tear gas blows and you have that red shit all over you and the money you stole. I checked the reports on the other robberies he pulled? Every one of them he said to the teller, no dye packs or that bait money with the registered serial numbers."

"Making conversation," Karen said, trying hard to maintain her composure. "People like to talk about what they do."

Daniel smiled.

And Karen said, "Carl's not your man."

"Tell me why you're so sure."

"I know him. He's a good guy."

"Karen, you hear yourself? You're telling me what you feel, not what you know. Tell me about *him*—you like the way he dances, what?"

Karen didn't answer that one. She wanted Daniel to leave her alone.

He said, "Okay, you want to put a wager on it, you say Tillman's clean?"

That brought her back, hooked her, and she said, "How much?"

"You lose, you go out dancing with me."

"Great. And if I'm right, what do I get?"

"My undying respect," Daniel said.

As soon as Karen got home she called her dad
at Marshall Sisco Investigations and told him about Carl Tillman, the robbery suspect in her life, and about Daniel Burdon's confident, condescending, smart-ass, irritating attitude.

Her dad said, "Is this guy colored?"

"Daniel?"

"I *know* he is. Friends of mine at Metro-Dade call him the
white man's Burdon, on account of he gets on their nerves always being right. I mean your guy. There's a running back in
the NFL named Tillman. I forget who he's with."

Karen said, "You're not helping any."

"The Tillman in the pros is colored—the reason I asked. I
think he's with the Bears."

"Carl's white."

"Okay, and you say you're crazy about him?"

"I like him, a lot."

"But you aren't sure he isn't doing the banks."

"I said I can't believe he is."

"Why don't you ask him?"

"Come on—if he is he's not gonna tell me."

"How do you know?"

She didn't say anything and after a few moments her dad
asked if she was still there.

"He's coming over tonight," Karen said.

"You want me to talk to him?"

"You're not serious."

"Then what'd you call me for?"

"I'm not sure what to do."

"Let the FBI work it."

"I'm supposed to be helping them."

"Yeah, but what good are you? You want to believe the guy's clean. Honey, the only way to find out if he is, you have to assume he isn't. You know what I'm saying? Why does a person rob banks? For money, yeah. But you have to be a moron, too, considering the odds against you, the security, cameras taking your picture. . . . So another reason could be the risk involved, it turns him on. The same reason he's playing around with you. . . ."

"He isn't playing around."

"I'm glad I didn't say 'sucking up to get information, see what you know.'"

"He's never mentioned banks." Karen paused. "Well, he might've once."

"You could bring it up, see how he reacts. He gets sweaty, call for backup. Look, whether he's playing around or loves you with all his heart, he's still risking twenty years. He doesn't know if you're onto him or not and that heightens the risk. It's like he thinks he's Cary Grant stealing jewels from the broad's home where he's having dinner, in his tux. But your guy's still a moron if he robs banks. You know all that. Your frame of mind, you just don't want to accept it."

"You think I should draw him out. See if I can set him up."

"Actually," her dad said, "I think you should find another boyfriend."

Karen remembered Christopher Walken in *The Dogs of War* placing his gun on a table in the front hall—the doorbell ringing—and laying a newspaper over the gun before he opened the door. She remembered it because at one time she was in love with Christopher Walken, not even caring that he wore his pants so high.

Carl reminded her some of Christopher Walken, the way he smiled with his eyes. He came a little after seven. Karen had on khaki shorts and a T-shirt, tennis shoes without socks.

"I thought we were going out."

They kissed and she touched his face, moving her hand lightly over his skin, smelling his aftershave, feeling the spot where his right earlobe was pierced.

"I'm making drinks," Karen said. "Let's have one and then I'll get ready." She started for the kitchen.

"Can I help?"

"You've been working all day. Sit down, relax."

It took her a couple of minutes. Karen returned to the living room with a drink in each hand, her leather bag hanging from her shoulder. "This one's yours." Carl took it and she dipped her shoulder to let the bag slip off and drop to the coffee table. Carl grinned.

"What've you got in there, a gun?"

"Two pounds of heavy metal. How was your day?"

They sat on the sofa and he told how it took almost four hours to land an eight-foot marlin, the leader wound around its bill. Carl said he worked his tail off hauling the fish aboard and the guy decided he didn't want it.

Karen said, "After you got back from Kendall?"

It gave him pause.

"Why do you think I was in Kendall?"

Carl had to wait while she sipped her drink.

"Didn't you stop by Florida Southern and withdraw twenty-eight hundred?"

That got him staring at her, but with no expression to speak of. Karen thinking, Tell me you were somewhere else and can prove it.

But he didn't; he kept staring.

"No dye packs, no bait money. Are you still seeing Kathy Lopez?"

Carl hunched over to put his drink on the coffee table and sat like that, leaning on his thighs, not looking at her now as Karen studied his profile, his elegant nose. She looked at his glass, his prints all over it, and felt sorry for him.

"Carl, you blew it."

He turned his head to look at her past his shoulder. He said, "I'm leaving," pushed up from the sofa and said, "If this is what you think of me . . ."

Karen said, "Carl, cut the shit," and put her drink down. Now, if he picked up her bag, that would cancel out any remaining doubts. She watched him pick up her bag. He got the Beretta out and let the bag drop.

"Carl, sit down. Will you, please?"

"I'm leaving. I'm walking out and you'll never see me again. But first . . ." He made her get a knife from the kitchen and cut the phone line in there and in the bedroom.

He *was* pretty dumb. In the living room again he said, "You know something? We could've made it."

Jesus. And he had seemed like such a cool guy. Karen watched him go to the front door and open it before turning to her again.

"How about letting me have five minutes? For old times' sake."

It was becoming embarrassing, sad. She said, "Carl, don't you understand? You're under arrest."

He said, "I don't want to hurt you, Karen, so don't try to stop me." He went out the door.

Karen walked over to the chest where she dropped her car keys and mail coming in the house: a bombé chest by the front door, the door still open. She laid aside the folded copy of the *Herald* she'd placed there, over her SIG Sauer, picked up the pistol, and went out to the front stoop, into the yellow glow of the porch light. She saw Carl at his car now, its white shape pale against the dark street, only about forty feet away.

"Carl, don't make it hard, okay?"

He had the car door open and half turned to look back. "I said I don't want to hurt you."

Karen said, "Yeah, well . . ." and raised the pistol to rack the slide and cupped her left hand under the grip. She said, "You move to get in the car, I'll shoot."

Carl turned his head again with a sad, wistful expression. "No you won't, sweetheart."

Don't say ciao, Karen thought. Please.

Carl said, "Ciao," turned to get in the car, and she shot him. Fired a single round at his left thigh and hit him where she'd aimed, in the fleshy part just below his butt. Carl howled and slumped inside against the seat and the steering wheel, his leg extended straight out, his hand gripping it, his eyes raised with a bewildered frown as Karen approached. The poor dumb guy looking at twenty years, and maybe a limp.

Karen felt she should say something. After all, for a few days there they were as intimate as two people can get. She thought about it for several moments, Carl staring up at her with rheumy eyes. Finally Karen said, "Carl, I want you to know I had a pretty good time, considering."

It was the best she could do.

HURRAH FOR
CAPT·EARLY

T he second banner said HERO OF SAN JUAN
HILL. Both were tied to the upstairs balcony
of the Congress Hotel and looked down on La
Salle Street in Sweetmary, a town named for a copper mine. The banners read across the building as
a single statement. The day that Captain Early
was expected home from the war in Cuba, over
now these two months, was October 10, 1898.

The manager of the hotel and one of his desk
clerks were the first to observe the colored man
who entered the lobby and dropped his bedroll on
the red velvet settee where it seemed he was about
to sit down. Bold as brass. A tall, well-built colored man wearing a suit of clothes that looked
new and appeared to fit him as though it might
possibly be his own and not one handed down to
him. He wore the suit, a stiff collar, and a necktie.
With the manager nearby but not yet aware of the
intruder, the young desk clerk spoke up, raised his
voice to tell the person, "You can't sit down
there."

The colored man turned his attention to the desk, taking a moment before he said, "Why is that?"

His quiet tone caused the desk clerk to hesitate and look over at the manager, who stood holding the day's mail, letters that had arrived on the El Paso & Southwestern morning run along with several guests now registered at the hotel and, apparently, this colored person. It was hard to tell his age, other than to say he was no longer a young man. He did seem clean and his bedroll was done up in bleached canvas.

"A hotel lobby," the desk clerk said, "is not a public place anyone can make theirself at home in. What is it you want here?"

At least he was uncovered, standing there now hat in hand. But then he said, "I'm waiting on Bren Early."

"*Bren* is it," the desk clerk said. "Captain Early's an acquaintance of yours?"

"We go way back a ways."

"You worked for him?"

"Some."

At this point the manager said, "We're all waiting for Captain Early. Why don't you go out front and watch for him?" Ending the conversation.

The desk clerk—his name was Monty—followed the colored man to the front entrance and stepped out on the porch to watch him, bedroll over his shoulder, walking south on La Salle the two short blocks to Fourth Street. Monty returned to the desk, where he said to the manager, "He walked right in the Gold Dollar."

The manager didn't look up from his mail.

Two riders from the Circle-Eye, a spread on the San Pedro that delivered beef to the mine company, were at a table with their glasses of beer: a rider named Macon and a rider named Wayman, young men who wore sweat-stained hats down on their eyes as they stared at the Negro. Right there, the bartender speaking to him as he poured a whiskey, still speaking as the colored man drank it and the bartender poured him another one. Macon asked Wayman if he had ever seen a nigger wearing a suit of clothes and a necktie. Wayman said he couldn't recall. When they finished drinking their beer and walked up to the bar, the colored man gone now, Macon asked the bartender who in the hell that smoke thought he was coming in here. "You would think," Macon said, "he'd go to one of the places where the miners drink."

The bartender appeared to smile, for some reason finding humor in Macon's remark. He said, "Boys, that was Bo Catlett. I imagine Bo drinks just about wherever he feels like drinking."

"Why?" Macon asked it, surprised. "He suppose to be somebody?"

"Bo lives up at White Tanks," the bartender told him, "at the Indin agency. Went to war and now he's home."

Macon squinted beneath the hat brim funneled low on his eyes. He said, "Nobody told me they was niggers in the war." Sounding as though it was the bartender's fault he hadn't been informed. When the bartender didn't add anything to help him out, Macon said, "Wayman's brother Wyatt was in the war, with Teddy Roosevelt's Rough Riders. Only, Wyatt didn't come home like the nigger."

Wayman, about eighteen years old, was nodding his head now.

Because nothing about this made sense to Macon, it was becoming an irritation. Again he said to Wayman, "You ever see a smoke wearing a suit of clothes like that?" He said, "Je-sus Christ."

Bo Catlett walked up La Salle Street favoring his left leg some, though the limp, caused by a Mauser bullet or by the regimental surgeon who cut it out of his hip, was barely noticeable. He stared at the sight of the mine works against the sky, ugly, but something monumental about it: straight ahead up the grade, the main shaft scaffolding and company buildings, the crushing mill lower down, ore tailings that humped this way in ridges on down the slope to run out at the edge of town. A sorry place, dark and forlorn; men walked up the grade from boardinghouses on Mill Street to spend half their life underneath the ground, buried before they were dead. Three whiskeys in him, Catlett returned to the hotel on the corner of Second Street, looked up at the sign that said HURRAH FOR CAPT. EARLY, and had to grin. THE HERO OF SAN JUAN HILL my ass.

Catlett mounted the steps to the porch, where he dropped his bedroll and took one of the rocking chairs all in a row, the porch empty, close on noon but nobody sitting out here, no drummers calling on La Salle Mining of New Jersey, the company still digging and scraping but running low on payload copper, operating only the day shift now. The rocking chairs, all dark green, needed painting. Man, but made of cane and comfortable with that nice squeak back and forth, back and forth. . . . Bo Catlett watched two riders coming this way up the street, couple of cowboys. . . . Catlett wondering how many times he had sat down in a real chair since April 25th when war was declared and he left Arizona to go looking for his old regiment, trailed them to Fort Assiniboine in the Department of the Dakotas, then clear across the country to Camp Chickamauga in Georgia and on down to Tampa where he caught up with them and Lieutenant John Pershing looked at his twenty-four years of service and put him up for squadron sergeant major. It didn't seem like any twenty-four years. . . .

Going back to when he joined the First Kansas Colored Volunteers in '63, age fifteen. Wounded at Honey Springs the same year. Guarded Rebel prisoners at Rock Island, took part in the occupation of Galveston. Then after the war got sent out here to join the all-Negro Tenth Cavalry on frontier station, Arizona Territory, and deal with hostile Apaches. In '87 went to Mexico with Lieutenant Brendan Early out of Fort Huachuca—Bren and a contract guide named Dana Moon, now the agent at the White Tanks reservation—brought back a one-eyed Mimbreño named Loco, brought back a white woman the renegade Apache had run off with—and Dana Moon later married—and they all got their pictures in some newspapers. Mustered out that same year, '87. . . . Drove a wagon for Capt. Early Hunting Expeditions Incorporated before going to work for Dana at White Tanks. He'd be sitting on Dana's porch this evening with a glass of mescal and Dana would say, "Well, now you've seen the elephant I don't imagine you'll want to stay around here." He'd tell Dana he saw the elephant a long time ago and wasn't too impressed. Just then another voice, not Dana's, said out loud to him:

"So you was in the war, huh?"

It was one of the cowboys. He sat his mount, a little clay-bank quarter horse, close to the porch rail, sat leaning on the pommel to show he was at ease, his hat low on his eyes, staring directly at Catlett in his rocking chair. The other one sat his mount, a bay, more out in the street, maybe holding back. This boy was not at ease but fidgety. Catlett remembered them in the Gold Dollar.

Now the one close said, "What was it you did over there in Cuba?"

Meaning a colored man. What did a colored man do. Like most people the boy not knowing anything about Negro soldiers in the war. This one squinting at him had size and maybe got his way enough he believed he could say whatever he pleased, or use a tone of voice that would irritate the person addressed. As he did just now.

"What did I do over there?" Catlett said. "What everybody did, I was in the war."

"You wrangle stock for the Rough Riders?"

"Where'd you get that idea?"

"I asked you a question. Is that what you did, tend their stock?"

Once Catlett decided to remain civil and maybe this boy would go away, he said, "There wasn't no stock. The Rough Riders, *even* the Rough Riders, were afoot. The only people had horses were artillery, pulling caissons with their Hotchkiss guns and the coffee grinders, what they called the

Gatling guns. Lemme see," Catlett said, "they had some mules, too, but I didn't tend anybody's stock."

"His brother was a Rough Rider," Macon said, raising one hand to hook his thumb at Wayman. "Served with Colonel Teddy Roosevelt and got killed in an ambush—the only way greasers know how to fight. I like to hear what you people were doing while his brother Wyatt was getting killed."

You people. Look at him trying to start a fight.

"You believe it was my fault he got killed?"

"I asked you what you were doing."

It wasn't even this kid's business. Catlett thinking, Well, see if you can educate him, and said, "Las Guásimas. You ever hear of it?"

The kid stared with his eyes half shut. Suspicious, or letting you know he's serious, Catlett thought. Keen-eyed and mean; you're not gonna put anything past him.

"What's it, a place over there?"

"That's right, Las Guásimas, the place where it happened. On the way to Santiago de Coo-ba. Sixteen men killed that day, mostly by rifle fire, and something like fifty wounded. Except it wasn't what you said, the dons pulling an ambush. It was more the Rough Riders walking along not looking where they was going."

The cowboy, Macon, said, "Je-sus Christ, you saying the Rough Riders didn't know what they were *do*ing?" Like this was something impossible to believe.

"They mighta had an idea *what* they was doing," Catlett said, "only thing it wasn't what they *shoulda* been doing." He said, "You understand the difference?" And thought, What're you explaining it to him for? The boy giving him that mean look again, ready to defend the Rough Riders. All right, he was so proud of Teddy's people, why hadn't he been over there with them?

"Look," Catlett said, using a quiet tone now, "the way it was, the dons had sharpshooters in these trees, a thicket of mangoes and palm trees growing wild you couldn't see into. You understand? Had men hidden in there were expert with the rifle, these Mausers they used with smokeless powder. Teddy's people come along a ridge was all covered with these trees and run into the dons, see, the dons letting some of the Rough Riders pass and then closing in on 'em. So, yeah, it was an ambush in a way." Catlett paused. "We was down on the road, once we caught up, moving in the same direction." He paused again, remembering something the cowboy said that bothered him. "There's nothing wrong with an ambush—like say you think it ain't *fair*? If you can set it up and keep your people behind cover, do it. There was a captain with the Rough Riders said he believed an officer should never take cover, should stand out there and be an example to his men. The captain said, 'There ain't a Spanish bullet made that can kill me.' Stepped out in the open and got shot in the head."

A couple of cowboys looking like the two who were mounted had come out of the Chinaman's picking their teeth and now stood by to see what was going on. Some people who had come out of the hotel were standing along the steps.

Catlett took all this in as he paused again, getting the words straight in his mind to tell how they left the road, some companies of the Tenth and the First, all regular army, went up the slope laying down fire and run off the dons before the

Rough Riders got cut to pieces, the Rough Riders volunteers and not experienced in all kind of situations—the reason they didn't know shit about advancing through hostile country or, get right down to it, what they were doing in Cuba, these people that come looking for glory and got served sharpshooters with Mausers and mosquitoes carrying yellow fever. Tell these cowboys the true story. General Wheeler, "Fightin' Joe" from the Confederate side in the Civil War now thirty-three years later an old man with a white beard; sees the Spanish pulling back at Las Guásimas and says, "Boys, we got the Yankees on the run." Man like that directing a battle. . . .

Tell the *whole* story if you gonna tell it, go back to sitting in the hold of the ship in Port Tampa a month, not allowed to go ashore for fear of causing incidents with white people who didn't want the men of the Tenth coming in their stores and cafés, running off their customers. Tell them—so we land in Cuba at a place called Daiquirí . . . saying in his mind then, Listen to me now. Was the Tenth at Daiquirí, the Ninth at Siboney. Experienced cavalry regiments that come off frontier station after thirty years dealing with hostile renegades, cutthroat horse thieves, reservation jumpers, land in Cuba and they put us to work unloading the ships while Teddy's people march off to meet the enemy and win some medals, yeah, and would've been wiped out at El Caney and on San Juan Hill if the colored boys hadn't come along and saved Colonel Teddy's ass and all his Rough Rider asses, showed them how to go up a hill and take a blockhouse. Saved them so the Rough Riders could become America's heroes.

All this in Bo Catlett's head and the banners welcoming Captain Early hanging over him.

One of the cowboys from the Chinaman's must've asked what was going on, because now the smart-aleck one brought his claybank around and began talking to them, glancing back at the porch now and again with his mean look. The two from the Chinaman's stood with their thumbs in their belts, while the mounted cowboy had his hooked around his suspenders now. None of them wore a gun belt or appeared to be armed. Now the two riders stepped down from their mounts and followed the other two along the street to a place called the Belle Alliance, a miners' saloon, and went inside.

Bo Catlett was used to mean dirty looks and looks of indifference, a man staring at him as though he wasn't even there. Now, the thing with white people, they had a hard time believing colored men fought in the war. You never saw a colored man on a U.S. Army recruiting poster or a picture of colored soldiers in newspapers. White people believed colored people could not be relied on in war. But why? There were some colored people that went out and killed wild animals, even lions, with a spear. No gun, a spear. And made hats out of the manes. See a colored man standing there in front of a lion coming at him fast as a train running downgrade, stands there with his spear, doesn't move, and they say colored men can't be relied on?

There was a story in newspapers how when Teddy Roosevelt was at the hill, strutting around in the open, he saw colored troopers going back to the rear and he drew his revolver and threatened to shoot them—till he found out they were going after ammunition. His own Rough Riders were pinned down in the guinea grass, the Spanish sharpshooters picking at them from up in the blockhouses. So the Tenth showed the white boys how to go up the hill angry, firing and yelling, making noise, set on driving the garlics clean from the hill. . . .

Found Bren Early and his company lying in the weeds, the scrub—that's all it was up that hill, scrub and sand, hard to get a footing in places; nobody ran all the way up, it was get up a ways and stop to fire, covering each other. Found Bren Early with a whistle in his mouth. He got up and started blowing it and waving his sword—come on, boys, to glory— and a Mauser bullet smacked him in the butt, on account of the way he was turned to his people, and Bren Early grunted, dropped his sword, and went down in the scrub to lay there cursing his luck, no doubt mortified to look like he got shot going the wrong way. Bo Catlett didn't believe Bren saw him pick up the sword. Picked it up, waved it at the Rough Riders and his Tenth Cav troopers, and they all went up that hill together, his troopers yelling, some of them singing, actually singing "They'll Be a Hot Time in the Old Town Tonight." Singing and shooting, honest to God, scaring the dons right out of their blockhouse. It was up on the crest Catlett got shot in his right hip and was taken to the Third Cav dressing station. It was set up on the Aguadores River at a place called "bloody ford," being it was under fire till the hill was captured. Catlett remembered holding on to the sword, tight, while the regimental surgeon dug the bullet out of him and he tried hard not to scream, biting his mouth till it bled. After, he was sent home and spent a month at Camp Wikoff, near Montauk out on Long Island, with a touch of yellow fever. Saw President McKinley when he came by September 3rd and made a speech, the President saying what they did over there in Cuba "commanded the unstinted praise of all your countrymen." Till he walked away from Montauk and came back into the world, Sergeant Major Catlett actually did believe he and the other members of the Tenth would be recognized as war heroes.

He wished Bren would hurry up and get here. He'd ask the hero of San Juan Hill how his heinie was and if he was getting much unstinted praise. If Bren didn't come pretty soon, Catlett decided, he'd see him another time. Get a horse out of the livery and ride it up White Tanks.

The four Circle-Eye riders sat at a front table in the Belle Alliance with a bottle of Green River whiskey, Macon staring out the window. The hotel was across the street and up the block a ways, but Macon could see it, the colored man in the suit of clothes still sitting on the porch, if he tilted his chair back and held on to the windowsill. He said, "No, sir, nobody told me they was niggers in the war."

Wayman said to the other two Circle-Eye riders, "Macon can't get over it."

Macon's gaze came away from the window. "It was *your* brother got killed."

Wayman said, "I know he did."

Macon said, "You don't care?"

The Circle-Eye riders watched him let his chair come down to hit the floor hard. They watched him get up without another word and walk out.

"I never thought much of coloreds," one of the Circle-Eye

riders said, "but you never hear me take on about 'em like Macon. What's his trouble?"

"I guess he wants to shoot somebody," Wayman said. "The time he shot that chili picker in Nogales? Macon worked his-self up to it the same way."

Catlett watched the one that was looking for a fight come out through the doors and go to the claybank, the reins looped once around the tie rail. He didn't touch the reins, though. What he did was reach into a saddlebag and bring out what Catlett judged to be a Colt .44 pistol. Right then he heard:

"Only guests of the hotel are allowed to sit out here."

Catlett watched the cowboy checking his loads now, turn-ing the cylinder of his six-shooter, the metal catching a glint of light from the sun, though the look of the pistol was dull and it appeared to be an old model.

Monty the desk clerk, standing there looking at Catlett without getting too close, said, "You'll have to leave. . . . Right now."

The cowboy was looking this way.

Making up his mind, Catlett believed. All right, now, yeah, he's made it up.

"Did you hear what I said?"

Catlett took time to look at Monty and then pointed off down the street. He said, "You see that young fella coming this way with the pistol? He think he like to shoot me. Say you don't allow people to sit here aren't staying at the ho-tel. How about, you allow them to get shot if they not a guest?"

He watched the desk clerk, who didn't seem to know whether to shit or go blind, eyes wide open, turn and run back in the lobby.

The cowboy, Macon, stood in the middle of the street now holding the six-shooter against his leg.

Catlett, still seated in the rocker, said, "You a mean rascal, ain't you? Don't take no sass, huh?"

The cowboy said something agreeing that Catlett didn't catch, the cowboy looking over to see his friends coming up the street now from the barroom. When he looked at the hotel porch again, Catlett was standing at the railing, his bedroll upright next to him leaning against it.

"I can be a mean rascal too," Catlett said, unbuttoning his suit coat. "I want you to know that before you take this too far. You understand?"

"You insulted Colonel Roosevelt and his Rough Riders," the cowboy said, "and you insulted Wayman's brother, killed in action over there in Cuba."

"How come," Catlett said, "you weren't there?"

"I was ready, don't worry, when the war ended. But we're talking about you. I say you're a dirty lying nigger and have no respect for people better'n you are. I want you to apologize to the colonel and his men and to Wayman's dead brother. . . ."

"Or what?" Catlett said.

"Answer to me," the cowboy said. "Are you armed? You aren't, you better get yourself a pistol."

"You want to shoot me," Catlett said, " 'cause I went to Cuba and you didn't?"

The cowboy was shaking his head. " 'Cause you lied. Have you got a pistol or not?"

Catlett said, "You calling me out, huh? You want us to fight a duel?"

" 'Less you apologize. Else get a pistol."

"But if I'm the one being called out, I have my choice of weapons, don't I? That's how I seen it work, twenty-four years in the U.S. Army in two wars. You hear what I'm saying?"

The cowboy was frowning now beneath his hat brim, squinting up at Bo Catlett. He said, "Pistols, it's what you use."

Catlett nodded. "If I say so."

"Well, what else is there?"

Confused and getting a mean look.

Catlett slipped his hand into the upright end of his bedroll and began to tug at something inside—the cowboy watching, the Circle-Eye riders in the street watching, the desk clerk and manager in the doorway and several hotel guests near them who had come out to the porch, all watching as Catlett drew a sword from the bedroll, a cavalry saber, the curved blade flashing as it caught the sunlight. He came past the people watching and down off the porch toward the cowboy in his hat and boots fixed with spurs that chinged as he turned to face Catlett, shorter than Catlett, appearing confused again holding the six-shooter at his side.

"If I choose to use sabers," Catlett said, "is that agreeable with you?"

"I don't have no *saber*."

Meanness showing now in his eyes.

"Well, you best get one."

"I never even had a sword in my hand."

Irritated. Drunk, too, his eyes not focusing as they should. Now he was looking over his shoulder at the Circle-Eye riders, maybe wanting them to tell him what to do.

One of them, not Wayman but one of the others, called out, "You got your forty-four in your hand, ain't you? What're you waiting on?"

Catlett raised the saber to lay the tip against Macon's breastbone, saying to him, "You use your pistol and I use steel? All right, if that's how you want it. See if you can shoot me 'fore this blade is sticking out your back. You game? . . . Speak up, boy."

In the hotel dining room having a cup of coffee, Catlett heard the noise outside, the cheering that meant Captain Early had arrived. Catlett waited. He wished one of the waitresses would refill his cup, but they weren't around now, nobody was. A half hour passed before Captain Early entered the dining room and came over to the table, leaving the people he was with. Catlett rose and they embraced, the hotel people and guests watching. It was while they stood this way that Bren saw, over Catlett's shoulder, the saber lying on the table, the curved steel on white linen. Catlett sat down. Bren looked closely at the saber's hilt. He picked it up and there was applause from the people watching. The captain bowed to them and sat down with the sergeant major.

"You went up the hill with this?"

"Somebody had to."

"I'm being recommended for a medal. 'For courage and pluck in continuing to advance under fire on the Spanish fortified position at the battle of Las Guásimas, Cuba, June 24th, 1898.' "

Catlett nodded. After a moment he said, "Will you tell me something? What was that war about?"

"You mean why'd we fight the dons?"

"Yeah, tell me."

"To free the oppressed Cuban people. Relieve them of Spanish domination."

"That's what I thought."

"You didn't know why you went to war?"

"I guess I knew," Catlett said. "I just wasn't sure."

THE TONTO WOMAN

A time would come, within a few years, when Ruben Vega would go to the church in Benson, kneel in the confessional, and say to the priest, "Bless me, Father, for I have sinned. It has been thirty-seven years since my last confession. . . . Since then I have fornicated with many women, maybe eight hundred. No, not that many, considering my work. Maybe six hundred only." And the priest would say, "Do you mean bad women or good women?" And Ruben Vega would say, "They are all good, Father." He would tell the priest he had stolen, in that time, about twenty thousand head of cattle but only maybe fifteen horses. The priest would ask him if he had committed murder. Ruben Vega would say no. "All that stealing you've done," the priest would say, "you've never killed anyone?" And Ruben Vega would say, "Yes, of course, but it was not to commit murder. You understand the distinction? Not to *kill* someone to take a life, but only to save my own."

Even in this time to come, concerned with dying in a state of sin, he would be confident. Ruben Vega knew himself, when he was right, when he was wrong.

Now, in a time before, with no thought of dying, but with the same confidence and caution that kept him alive, he watched a woman bathe. Watched from a mesquite thicket on the high bank of a wash.

She bathed at the pump that stood in the yard of the adobe, the woman pumping and then stooping to scoop the water from the basin of the irrigation ditch that led off to a vegetable patch of corn and beans. Her dark hair was pinned up in a swirl, piled on top of her head. She was bare to her gray skirt, her upper body pale white, glistening wet in the late afternoon sunlight. Her arms were very thin, her breasts small, but there they were with the rosy blossoms on the tips and Ruben Vega watched them as she bathed, as she raised one arm and her hand rubbed soap under the arm and down over her ribs. Ruben Vega could almost feel those ribs, she was so thin. He felt sorry for her, for all the women like her, stick women drying up in the desert, waiting for a husband to ride in smelling of horse and sweat and leather, lice living in his hair.

There was a stock tank and rickety windmill off in the pasture, but it was empty graze, all dust and scrub. So the man of the house had moved his cows to grass somewhere and would be coming home soon, maybe with his sons. The woman appeared old enough to have young sons. Maybe there was a little girl in the house. The chimney appeared cold. Animals stood in a mesquite-pole corral off to one side of the house, a cow and a calf and a dun-colored horse, that was all. There were a few chickens. No buckboard or wagon. No clothes drying on the line. A lone woman here at day's end.

From fifty yards he watched her. She stood looking this way now, into the red sun, her face raised. There was something strange about her face. Like shadow marks on it, though there was nothing near enough to her to cast shadows.

He waited until she finished bathing and returned to the house before he mounted his bay and came down the wash to the pasture. Now as he crossed the yard, walking his horse, she would watch him from the darkness of the house and make a judgment about him. When she appeared again it might be with a rifle, depending on how she saw him.

Ruben Vega said to himself, Look, I'm a kind person. I'm not going to hurt nobody.

She would see a bearded man in a cracked straw hat with the brim bent to his eyes. Black beard, with a revolver on his hip and another beneath the leather vest. But look at my eyes, Ruben Vega thought. Let me get close enough so you can see my eyes.

Stepping down from the bay he ignored the house, let the horse drink from the basin of the irrigation ditch as he pumped water and knelt to the wooden platform and put his mouth to the rusted pump spout. Yes, she was watching him. Looking up now at the doorway he could see part of her: a coarse shirt with sleeves too long and the gray skirt. He could see strands of dark hair against the whiteness of the shirt, but could not see her face.

As he rose, straightening, wiping his mouth, he said, "May we use some of your water, please?"

The woman didn't answer him.

He moved away from the pump to the hardpack, hearing the ching of his spurs, removed his hat and gave her a little bow. "Ruben Vega, at your service. Do you know Diego Luz, the horse-breaker?" He pointed off toward a haze of foothills. "He lives up there with his family and delivers horses to the big ranch, the Circle-Eye. Ask Diego Luz, he'll tell you I'm a person of trust." He waited a moment. "May I ask how you're called?" Again he waited.

"You watched me," the woman said.

Ruben Vega stood with his hat in his hand facing the woman, who was half in shadow in the doorway. He said, "I waited. I didn't want to frighten you."

"You watched me," she said again.

"No, I respect your privacy."

She said, "The others look. They come and watch."

He wasn't sure who she meant. Maybe anyone passing by. He said, "You see them watching?"

She said, "What difference does it make?" She said then, "You come from Mexico, don't you?"

"Yes, I was there. I'm here and there, working as a drover." Ruben Vega shrugged. "What else is there to do, uh?" Showing her he was resigned to his station in life.

"You'd better leave," she said.

When he didn't move, the woman came out of the doorway into light and he saw her face clearly for the first time. He felt a shock within him and tried to think of something to say, but could only stare at the blue lines tattooed on her face: three straight lines on each cheek that extended from her cheekbones to her jaw, markings that seemed familiar, though he could not in this moment identify them.

He was conscious of himself standing in the open with nothing to say, the woman staring at him with curiosity, as though wondering if he would hold her gaze and look at her. Like there was nothing unusual about her countenance. Like it was common to see a woman with her face tattooed and you might be expected to comment, if you said anything at all, "Oh, that's a nice design you have there. Where did you have it done?" That would be one way—if you couldn't say something interesting about the weather or about the price of cows in Benson.

Ruben Vega, his mind empty of pleasantries, certain he would never see the woman again, said, "Who did that to you?"

She cocked her head in an easy manner, studying him as he studied her, and said, "Do you know, you're the first person who's come right out and asked."

"Mojave," Ruben Vega said, "but there's something different. Mojaves tattoo their chins only, I believe."

"And look like they were eating berries," the woman said. "I told them if you're going to do it, do it all the way. Not like a blue dribble."

It was in her eyes and in the tone of her voice, a glimpse of the rage she must have felt. No trace of fear in the memory, only cold anger. He could hear her telling the Indians—this skinny woman, probably a girl then—until they did it her way and marked her good for all time. Imprisoned her behind the blue marks on her face.

"How old were you?"

"You've seen me and had your water," the woman said, "now leave."

It was the same type of adobe house as the woman's but with a great difference. There was life here, the warmth of family: children sleeping now, Diego Luz's wife and her mother cleaning up after the meal as the two men sat outside in horsehide chairs and smoked and looked at the night. At one time they had both worked for a man named Sundeen and packed running irons to vent the brands on the cattle they stole. Ruben Vega was still an outlaw, in his fashion, while Diego Luz broke green horses and sold them to cattle companies.

They sat at the edge of the ramada, an awning made of mesquite, and stared at pinpoints of light in the universe. Ruben Vega asked about the extent of graze this season, where the large herds were that belonged to the Maricopa and the Circle-Eye. He had been thinking of cutting out maybe a hundred—he wasn't greedy—and driving them south to sell to the mine companies. He had been scouting the Circle-Eye range, he said, when he came to the strange woman. . . .

The Tonto woman, Diego Luz said. Everyone called her that now.

Yes, she had been living there, married a few years, when she went to visit her family, who lived on the Gila above

Painted Rock. Well, some Yavapai came looking for food. They clubbed her parents and two small brothers to death and took the girl north with them. The Yavapai traded her to the Mojave as a slave. . . .

"And they marked her," Ruben Vega said.

"Yes, so when she died the spirits would know she was Mojave and not drag her soul down into a rathole," Diego Luz said.

"Better to go to heaven with your face tattooed," Ruben Vega said, "than not at all. Maybe so."

During a drought the Mojave traded her to a band of Tonto Apaches for two mules and a bag of salt and one day she appeared at Bowie with the Tontos that were brought in to be sent to Oklahoma. Among the desert Indians twelve years and returned home last spring.

"It put age on her," Ruben Vega said. "But what about her husband?"

"Her husband? He banished her," Diego Luz said, "like a leper. Unclean from living among the red niggers. No one speaks of her to him, it isn't allowed."

Ruben Vega frowned. There was something he didn't understand. He said, "Wait a minute—"

And Diego Luz said, "Don't you know who her husband is? Mr. Isham himself, man, of the Circle-Eye. She comes home to find her husband a rich man. He don't live in that hut no more. No, he owns a hundred miles of graze and a house it took them two years to build, the glass and bricks brought in by the Southern Pacific. Sure, the railroad comes and he's a rich cattleman in only a few years."

"He makes her live there alone?"

"She's his wife, he provides for her. But that's all. Once a month his segundo named Bonnet rides out there with supplies and has someone shoe her horse and look at the animals."

"But to live in the desert," Ruben Vega said, still frowning, thoughtful, "with a rusty pump . . ."

"Look at her," Diego Luz said. "What choice does she have?"

It was hot down in this scrub pasture, a place to wither and die. Ruben Vega loosened the new willow-root straw that did not yet conform to his head, though he had shaped the brim to curve down on one side and rise slightly on the other so that the brim slanted across the vision of his left eye. He held on his lap a nearly flat cardboard box that bore the name L.S. WEISS MERCANTILE STORE.

The woman gazed up at him, shading her eyes with one hand. Finally she said, "You look different."

"The beard began to itch," Ruben Vega said, making no mention of the patches of gray he had studied in the hotel-room mirror. "So I shaved it off." He rubbed a hand over his jaw and smoothed down the tips of his mustache that was still full and seemed to cover his mouth. When he stepped down from the bay and approached the woman standing by the stick-fence corral, she looked off into the distance and back again.

She said, "You shouldn't be here."

Ruben Vega said, "Your husband doesn't want nobody to look at you. Is that it?" He held the store box, waiting for her to answer. "He has a big house with trees and the San Pedro River in his yard. Why doesn't he hide you there?"

She looked off again and said, "If they find you here, they'll shoot you."

"They," Ruben Vega said. "The ones who watch you bathe? Work for your husband and keep more than a close eye on you, and you'd like to hit them with something, wipe the grins from their faces."

"You better leave," the woman said.

The blue lines on her face were like claw marks, though not as wide as fingers: indelible lines of dye etched into her flesh with a cactus needle, the color worn and faded but still vivid against her skin, the blue matching her eyes.

He stepped close to her, raised his hand to her face, and touched the markings gently with the tips of his fingers, feeling nothing. He raised his eyes to hers. She was staring at him. He said, "You're in there, aren't you? Behind these little bars. They don't seem like much. Not enough to hold you."

She said nothing, but seemed to be waiting.

He said to her, "You should brush your hair. Brush it every day. . . ."

"Why?" the woman said.

"To feel good. You need to wear a dress. A little parasol to match."

"I'm asking you to leave," the woman said. But didn't move from his hand, with its yellowed, stained nails, that was like a fist made of old leather.

"I'll tell you something if I can," Ruben Vega said. "I know women all my life, all kinds of women in the way they look and dress, the way they adorn themselves according to custom. Women are always a wonder to me. When I'm not with a woman I think of them as all the same because I'm thinking of one thing. You understand?"

"Put a sack over their head," the woman said.

"Well, I'm not thinking of what she looks like then, when I'm out in the mountains or somewhere," Ruben Vega said. "That part of her doesn't matter. But when I'm *with* the woman, ah, then I realize how they are all different. You say, of course. This isn't a revelation to you. But maybe it is when you think about it some more."

The woman's eyes changed, turned cold. "You want to go to bed with me? Is that what you're saying, why you bring a gift?"

He looked at her with disappointment, an expression of weariness. But then he dropped the store box and took her to him gently, placing his hands on her shoulders, feeling her small bones in his grasp as he brought her in against him and his arms went around her.

He said, "You're gonna die here. Dry up and blow away."

She said, "Please . . ." Her voice hushed against him.

"They wanted only to mark your chin," Ruben Vega said, "in the custom of those people. But you wanted your own marks, didn't you? *Your* marks, not like anyone else. . . . Well, you got them." After a moment he said to her, very quietly, "Tell me what you want."

The hushed voice close to him said, "I don't know."

He said, "Think about it and remember something. There is no one else in the world like you."

He reined the bay to move out and saw the dust trail rising out of the old pasture, three riders coming, and heard the woman say, "I told you. Now it's too late."

A man on a claybank and two young riders eating his dust,

finally separating to come in abreast, reined to a walk as they reached the pump and the irrigation ditch. The woman, walking from the corral to the house, said to them, "What do you want? I don't need anything, Mr. Bonnet."

So this would be the Circle-Eye foreman on the claybank. The man ignored her, his gaze holding on Ruben Vega with a solemn expression, showing he was going to be dead serious. A chew formed a lump in his jaw. He wore army suspenders and sleeve garters, his shirt buttoned up at the neck. As old as you are, Ruben Vega thought, a man who likes a tight feel of security and is serious about his business.

Bonnet said to him finally, "You made a mistake."

"I don't know the rules," Ruben Vega said.

"She told you to leave her be. That's the only rule there is. But you bought yourself a dandy new hat and come back here."

"That's some hat," one of the young riders said. This one held a single-shot Springfield across his pommel. The foreman, Bonnet, turned in his saddle and said something to the other rider, who unhitched his rope and began shaking out a loop, hanging it nearly to the ground.

It's a show, Ruben Vega thought. He said to Bonnet, "I was leaving."

Bonnet said, "Yes, indeed, you are. On the off end of a rope. We're gonna drag you so you'll know the ground and never cross this land again."

The rider with the Springfield said, "Gimme your hat, mister, so's you don't get it dirty."

At this point Ruben Vega nudged his bay and began moving in on the foreman, who straightened, looking over at the roper, and said, "Well, tie on to him."

But Ruben Vega was close to the foreman now, the bay taller than the claybank, and would move the claybank if the man on his back told him to. Ruben Vega watched the fore-man's eyes moving and knew the roper was coming around behind him. Now the foreman turned his head to spit and let go a stream that spattered the hardpack close to the bay's forelegs.

"Stand still," Bonnet said, "and we'll get her done easy. Or you can run and get snubbed out of your chair. Either way."

Ruben Vega was thinking that he could drink with this ramrod and they'd tell each other stories until they were drunk. The man had thought it would be easy: chase off a Mexican gunnysacker who'd come sniffing the boss's wife. A kid who was good with a rope and another one who could shoot cans off the fence with an old Springfield should be enough.

Ruben Vega said to Bonnet, "Do you know who I am?"

"Tell us," Bonnet said, "so we'll know what the cat drug in and we drug out."

And Ruben Vega said, because he had no choice, "I hear the rope in the air, the one with the rifle is dead. Then you. Then the roper."

His words drew silence because there was nothing more to be said. In the moments that Ruben Vega and the one named Bonnet stared at each other, the woman came out to them holding a revolver, an old Navy Colt, which she raised and laid the barrel against the muzzle of the foreman's claybank.

She said, "Leave now, Mr. Bonnet, or you'll walk nine miles to shade."

There was no argument, little discussion, a few grumbling words. The Tonto woman was still Mrs. Isham. Bonnet rode away with his young hands and a new silence came over the yard.

Ruben Vega said, "He believes you'd shoot his horse."

The woman said, "He believes I'd cut steaks, and eat it too. It's how I'm seen after twelve years of that other life."

Ruben Vega began to smile. The woman looked at him and in a few moments she began to smile with him. She shook her head then, but continued to smile. He said to her, "You could have a good time if you want to."

She said, "How, scaring people?"

He said, "If you feel like it." He said, "Get the present I brought you and open it."

He came back for her the next day in a Concord buggy, wearing his new willow-root straw and a cutaway coat over his revolvers, the coat he'd rented at a funeral parlor. Mrs. Isham wore the pale blue-and-white lace-trimmed dress he'd bought at Weiss's store, sat primly on the bustle, and held the parasol against the afternoon sun all the way to Benson, ten miles, and up the main street to the Charles Crooker Hotel where the drummers and cattlemen and railroad men sitting in their front-porch rockers stared and stared.

They walked past the manager and into the dining room before Ruben Vega removed his hat and pointed to the table he liked, one against the wall between two windows. The waitress in her starched uniform was wide-eyed taking them over and getting them seated. It was early and the dining room was not half filled.

"The place for a quiet dinner," Ruben Vega said. "You see how quiet it is?"

"Everybody's looking at me," Sarah Isham said to the menu in front of her.

Ruben Vega said, "I thought they were looking at me. All right, soon they'll be used to it."

She glanced up and said, "People are leaving."

He said, "That's what you do when you finish eating, you leave."

She looked at him, staring, and said, "Who are you?"

"I told you."

"Only your name."

"You want me to tell you the truth, why I came here?"

"Please."

"To steal some of your husband's cattle."

She began to smile and he smiled. She began to laugh and he laughed, looking openly at the people looking at them, but not bothered by them. Of course they'd look. How could they help it? A Mexican rider and a woman with blue stripes on her face sitting at a table in the hotel dining room, laughing. He said, "Do you like fish? I know your Indian brothers didn't serve you none. It's against their religion. Some things are for religion, as you know, and some things are against it. We spend all our lives learning customs. Then they change them. I'll tell you something else if you promise not to be angry or point your pistol at me. Something else I could do the rest of my life. I could look at you and touch you and love you."

Her hand moved across the linen tablecloth to his with the cracked, yellowed nails and took hold of it, clutched it.

She said, "You're going to leave."

He said, "When it's time."

She said, "I know you. I don't know anyone else."

He said, "You're the loveliest woman I've ever met. And the strongest. Are you ready? I think the man coming now is your husband."

It seemed strange to Ruben Vega that the man stood looking at him and not at his wife. The man seemed not too old for her, as he had expected, but too self-important. A man with a very serious demeanor, as though his business had failed or someone in his family had passed away. The man's wife was still clutching the hand with the gnarled fingers. Maybe that was it. Ruben Vega was going to lift her hand from his, but then thought, Why? He said as pleasantly as he was able, "Yes, can I help you?"

Mr. Isham said, "You have one minute to mount up and ride out of town."

"Why don't you sit down," Ruben Vega said, "have a glass of wine with us?" He paused and said, "I'll introduce you to your wife."

Sarah Isham laughed; not loud but with a warmth to it and Ruben Vega had to look at her and smile. It seemed all right to release her hand now. As he did he said, "Do you know this gentleman?"

"I'm not sure I've had the pleasure," Sarah Isham said. "Why does he stand there?"

"I don't know," Ruben Vega said. "He seems worried about something."

"I've warned you," Mr. Isham said. "You can walk out or be dragged out."

Ruben Vega said, "He has something about wanting to drag people. Why is that?" And again heard Sarah's laugh, a giggle now that she covered with her hand. Then she looked up at her husband, her face with its blue tribal lines raised to the soft light of the dining room.

She said, "John, look at me. . . . Won't you please sit with us?"

Now it was as if the man had to make a moral decision, first consult his conscience, then consider the manner in which he would pull the chair out—the center of attention. When finally he was seated, upright on the chair and somewhat away from the table, Ruben Vega thought, All that to sit down. He felt sorry for the man now, because the man was not the kind who could say what he felt.

Sarah said, "John, can you look at me?"

He said, "Of course I can."

"Then do it. I'm right here."

"We'll talk later," her husband said.

She said, "When? Is there a visitor's day?"

"You'll be coming to the house, soon."

"You mean to see it?"

"To live there."

She looked at Ruben Vega with just the trace of a smile, a sad one. Then said to her husband, "I don't know if I want to. I don't know you. So I don't know if I want to be married to you. Can you understand that?"

Ruben Vega was nodding as she spoke. He could understand it. He heard the man say, "But we *are* married. I have an obligation to you and I respect it. Don't I provide for you?"

Sarah said, "Oh, my God—" and looked at Ruben Vega. "Did you hear that? He provides for me." She smiled again, not able to hide it, while her husband began to frown, confused.

"He's a generous man," Ruben Vega said, pushing up from the table. He saw her smile fade, though something warm remained in her eyes. "I'm sorry. I have to leave. I'm going on a trip tonight, south, and first I have to pick up a few things." He moved around the table to take one of her hands in his, not caring what the husband thought. He said, "You'll do all right, whatever you decide. Just keep in mind there's no one else in the world like you."

She said, "I can always charge admission. Do you think ten cents a look is too high?"

"At least that," Ruben Vega said. "But you'll think of something better."

He left her there in the dining room of the Charles Crooker Hotel in Benson, Arizona—maybe to see her again sometime, maybe not—and went out with a good conscience to take some of her husband's cattle.

TENKILLER

I.

At Kim's funeral—people coming up to Ben with their solemn faces—he couldn't help thinking of what his granddad Carl had said to him fifteen years ago, that he hoped Ben would have better luck with women.

"We seem to have 'em around for a year or so," the old man said, "and they take off or die on us."

It was on Ben's mind today, along with a feeling of expectation he couldn't help. Here he was standing ten feet from the open casket, Kim in there with her blond hair sprayed for maybe the first time, her lips sealed, a girl he lived with and loved, and he was anxious to take off. Go home as a different person. Maybe look up a girl named Denise he used to know, if she was still around. Get away from the movie business for a while.

He could've taken 40, a clear shot across the entire Southwest from L.A. to Okmulgee, Oklahoma, fourteen hundred miles, but took 10 instead, drove four hundred miles out of his way to look in on the Professional Bull Riders Bud Light World Challenge in Austin. Getting away was the main thing; there was no hurry to get home.

He thought he might see some of his old buddies hanging around the chutes, not a one Ben's age still riding. Get up in your thirties and have any brains you were through with bulls. Ben entered the working end of the arena to the smell of livestock, got as far as the pens shaking hands and was taken up to the broadcast booth. An old guy he remembered as Owen still calling the rides.

Owen said, "Folks," taking the mike from its stand as he got up, "we have a surprise visitor showed up, former world champion bull rider Ben Webster, out of Okmulgee, Oklahoma." He said, "Ben, I liked to not recognize you without your hat on. Man, all that hair—you gone Hollywood on us or what?" Owen straight-faced, having fun with him.

Ben slipped his sunglasses off saying yeah, well, he'd been working out there the past ten years, getting by.

"Your name still comes up," Owen said. "I see a young rider shows some style, I wonder could he be another Ben Webster. I won't say you made it look easy, but you sure sat a bull, and didn't appear to get off till you felt like it. Listen, I want to hear what you been doing in Hollywood, but right now, folks, we got Stubby Dobbs, a hundred and thirty-five pounds of cowboy astride a two-thousand-pound Brahma name of Nitro." Owen turned to the TV monitor. "You see Stubby wrapping his bull rope good and tight. Ben, you don't want your hand to slip out of there during a ride."

"You're gone if it does," Ben said.

He had taken Kim to a rodeo in Las Vegas, explained how you had to stay on the bull eight seconds holding on with one hand, and you can't touch the bull with your other hand, and she said, "Eight seconds, that's all? Hell." He told her she might last a second or two, being athletic. Kim said, "Bring it on," waving both hands toward her body, "I'll ride him." He'd miss the way things he said to her could become fighting words.

"All right," Owen was saying, "I believe Stubby's ready, tugging his hat down . . . And here we go, folks, Stubby Dobbs out of Polson, Montana, on Nitro. Ride him, Stubby."

Ben watched the butternut bull come humping out of the gate like he had a cow's butt under him, humping and bucking, wanting this boy off his back in a hurry, the bull throwing his hindquarters in the air now with a hard twist, Nitro humping and twisting in a circle, Stubby's free hand reaching out for balance, the bull humping and twisting his "caboose," Owen called it, right up to the buzzer and Stubby let go to be flung in the air, whipped from the bull to land hard in the arena dirt.

"Well, you can hear the crowd liked that ride," Owen said, "it was a good'n. But it looks like Stubby's favoring his shoulder."

Stubby holding one arm tight to his body and looking back as he scurried to safety, the rodeo clowns heading Nitro for the exit gate, Ben thinking: Don't look back. You're a bull rider, boy, get some strut in your gait. Check the rodeo bunnies in the first row and tip your hat.

"You can ride to the buzzer," Owen was telling the crowd, "and still get in trouble on your dis-mount. Ben, I imagine you had your share of injuries."

"The usual, separated shoulders, busted collarbone. That padded vest is good for sponsor decals but that's about all."

"You think riders'll ever have to wear helmets?"

Ben said, "Owen, the day they won't let you wear your cowboy hat, there won't be anybody riding bulls."

"I know what you mean," Owen said. "Well, I thought Stubby rode that train to score a good ninety points or better. How did you see he did, Ben?"

They were waiting for the number to show on the monitor.

"I think the judges'll give Stubby his ride," Ben said, "but won't think as much of that bull. He hasn't learned all the dirty tricks yet, kept humping in the same direction. I'd have to score it an eighty-five."

And there it was on the monitor, eighty-five, Owen saying, "Well, Ben Webster still knows his bulls." Owen was looking toward the stalls now, saying that while the next rider was getting ready they'd take a commercial break. Owen turned off his mike and said to Ben, "Come on sit down. I want to hear some of the movies you were in."

"I was in *Dances with Wolves,* my first picture."

"What were you in it? I don't recall seeing you."

"I was a Lakota Sioux. Got shot off my horse by a Yankee soldier. I was in *Braveheart.* Took an arrow in the chest and went off the horse's rump. *Die Hard with a Vengeance* I wrecked cars. I got shot in *Air Force One,* run through with a sword in *The Mask of Zorro.* I got stepped on in *Godzilla,* in a car. Let's see, I was in *Independence Day . . .*"

"Yeah . . . ?"

"*Last Action Hero, Rising Sun, Black Rain . . . Terminal Velocity*. Others I can't think of offhand."

"I missed some of them," Owen said. "I was wondering, all those movies, you have a big part in any of 'em?"

"I'm a stuntman, Owen. They learn you rode bulls, you're hired."

A kid from Brazil named Adriano rode a couple of bulls that hated him and were mature and had all the moves—one of them called Dillinger, last year's bull of the year—and the kid hung on to take the $75,000 purse. Seventy-five grand for sitting on bulls for sixteen seconds.

Ben picked up three cases of Bud, a cold six-pack and a bag of ice for his cooler at the drive-thru Party Barn and aimed his black Mercedes SUV north toward Dallas, two hundred miles. He'd cross the Oklahoma line and head for McAlester, home of the state prison he used to visit with his granddad, Carl, and then on up to Okmulgee, the whole trip close to four-fifty—get home at three A.M. No, he'd better stop at a motel the other side of Dallas, take his time in the morning and get there about noon. Drive through town, see if it had changed any. The last time he was home, seven years ago, was for his granddad's funeral. Carl Webster, who'd raised him, dead at eighty.

Ben was thinking, sixteen into seventy-five thousand was around . . . forty-five hundred a second, about what you got for smashing up a car. He had earned $485,342 less expenses his last year of bull riding, way more than he ever made in a year doing stunt gags.

The six-pack was in the cooler behind his seat, a cold Bud wedged between his thighs, Ben following his high beams into the dark listening to country on the radio. The three cases of beer were in the far back with his stuff: travel bags full of clothes, coats on hangers, four pair of boots—two of them worn out but would break his heart to get rid of. He had boxes of photographs back there, movie videos, books . . .

One of the books, written before Ben was born, was a volume of Oklahoma history called *Hell Raisin' Days* that covered a period from the 1870s to the Second World War. Ben's grandfather and great-grandfather were both in the book. He had told Kim about them.

How Virgil Webster, his great-granddad, was born in Oklahoma when it was Indian Territory, his mother part Northern Cheyenne. Virgil was a marine on the battleship *Maine* when she blew up in Havana Harbor, February 15, 1898. He survived to fight in the Spanish-American War, was wounded, married a girl named Graciaplena in Cuba, and came home to buy a section of land that had pecan trees on it. Inside of twenty years Virgil had almost twelve hundred acres planted in pecans and another section used to graze cattle he bought, fed and sold. Finding oil under his land and leasing a piece of it to a drilling company made Virgil a pile of money and he built a big house on the property. He said they could pump all the oil they wanted, which they did, he'd still have his pe-cans.

Ben's granddad Carl, Virgil's only son, shot a cattle thief riding off with some of their stock when he was fifteen years old. Hit him with a Winchester at a good four hundred yards. He was christened Carlos Huntington Webster, named for his mother's dad in Cuba and a Colonel Robert Huntington, Virgil's commanding officer in the marines when they took Guantánamo, but came to use only part of the name.

Once Carlos joined the Marshals Service in 1927 everybody began calling him Carl; he was stubborn about answering to it but finally went along, seeing the name as short for Carlos. By the 1930s, he had become legendary as one of Oklahoma's most colorful lawmen. There were newspaper stories that described Carl Webster being on intimate terms with girlfriends of well-known desperadoes from Frank Miller to George "Machine Gun" Kelly.

Ben showed Kim photos of his mother and dad, Cheryl and Robert, taken in California sunshine, his dad in uniform, but said he had no memory of them. Robert, a career marine, was killed in Vietnam in '68 during Tet, when Ben was three years old. Cheryl gave him up to become a hippie, went to San Francisco and died there of drugs and alcohol. It was how Carl, sixty-two at the time and retired from the Marshals, came to raise him. Kim would ask about Cheryl, wanting to know how a mother could give up her little boy, but Ben didn't have the answer. He said Carl would tell him about his dad, how Robert was a tough kid, hardheaded and liked to fight, joined the marines on account of Virgil telling him stories when he was a kid, and was a DI at Pendleton before going to Vietnam.

"But he'd never say much about my mother other than she was sick all the time. I guess she took up serious drugs and that was that."

Actually, Ben said, Carl didn't talk much about any of the women in the family. "Not until I dropped out of Tulsa after a couple of years to get my rodeo ticket and we sat down with a fifth of Jim Beam."

He told Kim some of what he remembered of the conversation. Carl, close to eighty at the time, saying the men in the family never had much luck with women. Even Virgil, came back from Cuba and never saw his mother again. She'd gone off to live on the Northern Cheyenne reservation, out at Lame Deer, Montana. Carl said he came out of his own mother, Ben's great-grandma Grace, bless her heart, and she was already dying from birthing him.

Carl said that time, "Now your grandma Kitty—I can barely remember her face even though I'm still married to the woman. If she died I doubt she's in Heaven. Boy, Kitty was hot stuff, wore those real skimpy dresses. She'd read about me in the paper and pretend to shiver in a cute way."

It sounded to Ben like Carl's idea was to take Kitty out of the honky-tonks and show her a happy home life. Only Kitty found herself living with a couple of guys who dipped Copenhagen, drank a lot, argued and took turns telling stories about fighting the dons in Cuba and chasing after outlaws in Oklahoma. "Kitty saw me as a geezer before my time," Carl said. "She had Robert, and took off and I never went looking for her."

This was the occasion Carl said to Ben, "I hope you have better luck with women. We seem to have 'em around for a year or so and they take off or die on us."

Kim said, "What's that supposed to mean, a curse?" She said, "Luck has nothing to do with it," starting to show some temper. "You know what your granddad's problem was? He saw himself as a ladies' man without knowing a goddamn thing about women. It was all guy stuff with Carl, and you ate it up. My Lord, raised by an old man with guns and livestock out in the middle of nowhere. Having a jarhead drill instructor for a dad wouldn't have helped either, even if you never met him. To tell you the truth," she said, "I'm surprised you're considerate and know how to please a woman."

They'd argue over dumb things like how to make chili and Kim would say, "I'm from where they invented it, for Christ sake, hon. We do certain things my way or I'm out of here. Like Kitty, or whatever her name was, your grandma."

This Kim Hunter, from Del Rio, Texas, down on the border, had come to Hollywood hoping to be a movie star and was told she'd have to change her name, as there already was a Kim Hunter. This Kim Hunter said, "Have the other one change hers," like she'd never seen her in *Streetcar* playing Marlon Brando's wife. She was a physical fitness nut and got into stunt work falling off horses, getting pushed out of moving cars, jumping off the *Titanic,* stepping in to get beat up in the same dress the star was wearing . . .

He said, "You think you'll ever leave me?"

She said, "I doubt it."

Their arguments played like scenes they could turn on and off. Their home in Studio City was aluminum siding with a flagstone patio, a lot of old shrubbery in the backyard and bats that would come in the house through the chimney.

Three weeks ago they'd spent Sunday on the beach at Point Dume, where Charlton Heston kisses the real Kim Hunter playing a monkey chick in *Planet of the Apes,* and she doesn't want to kiss him because being a human he's so ugly—right before he takes off and comes to the head of the Statue of Liberty sticking out of the sand.

"You'd never catch me playing an ape," Kim said.

That day they walked along the edge of the Pacific Ocean talking about getting married and spending the rest of their lives together.

"You sure you want to?"

Ben said, "Yeah, I'm sure."

"If we're gonna have any children—"

"I know, and I want kids. Really."

They had fallen in love falling off a ladder in a movie, five takes, and were still in love almost two years later. She was slim and liked to wear hiking boots with print dresses.

Crossing the rocks to the path up the cliff—that bed of volcanic rock at Point Dume—Kim twisted her ankle. They got home, she put ice on it and an Ace wrap and said she was fine. They had talked about going to a movie that night, *Harry Potter* or *Ocean's Eleven.* Kim said no problem, she was up for it, and said, "You promised to fix the chimney today."

Ben was in the kitchen adding mushrooms to the Paul Newman spaghetti sauce. He said, "In a minute."

She limped out saying she'd take care of it, not sounding

mad or upset; it was just that impulsive way she had. He called to her to wait. "Can't you wait one minute?" No answer from outside. If she thought she could do it—she had done enough climbing and falling gags, she knew how. He thought of the day they fell off the ladder together five times in the LONG SHOT of the couple eloping . . . and now they were getting married. He told Kim and told himself he was all for it and believed he meant it.

She had dragged the ladder out of the garage, laid it against the chimney to climb up and replace the screen over the opening so the bats would quit flying in. She must've got right to the top. . . . He heard her scream and found her at the foot of the ladder, on the flagstone.

For the next three days and nights he sat close to the hospital bed taking her hand, touching her face, asking her to please open her eyes. He prayed, having once been a Baptist, see if it would do any good, but she died as he watched her and had to be told by the nurse she was gone.

They let him sit there while he tried to place the blame somewhere, going through *ifs.*

If he had quit slicing the mushrooms right away.

If Kim wasn't so—the way she was.

If they hadn't gone to Point Dume she wouldn't have twisted her ankle. He was sure it was the ankle caused her to fall.

That evening at home he got out the Jim Beam and it reminded him of his granddad that last time they were together, Carl hoping Ben had better luck with women, having 'em around a year or so and "they take off or die on us."

He tried to find a way to blame Carl for telling him that,

Ben now looking at four generations of bad luck with women. He was afraid it meant that if it wasn't Kim's time had come it would've been some other girl's.

The idea was in his head now, stuck there. He didn't see it as a curse; there was no such thing. Still, there it was and he had to ask himself, You think you can handle it?

They had talked about taking a trip one of these days to show each other where they came from, Kim saying, "A bull rider, I imagine you'll show me a stock tank on a feed lot, like you're proud of it."

Turning off the highway into Okmulgee he was thinking this could be his part of the tour, Kim sitting next to him in her denim jacket, Ben in a wool shirt hanging out of his Levi's. It was mid-November, the best time of the year to show off his land. They'd be harvesting the pecans and Lydell, his caretaker-foreman, would have a crew out shaking the trees and gathering up the nuts. First, though, a tour through town. And right away he was thinking of Denise again, Denise appearing in his mind ever since he left L.A.

Okmulgee, population: 13,022.

Show Kim some history, the Creek Nation Council House, and tell her about the "Trail of Tears" and how Cherokees and Chickasaws and Creeks were forced to move here from Eastern states. He'd be serious about it and she wouldn't say anything. He was surprised to see a brand-new jail next to the county courthouse.

Here was a chance to tell about Denise if he wanted to. Say to Kim, "See the courthouse? That whole top floor used to be the jail. I spent a night there when a girl named Denise got me in trouble." Kim would want to know about it. He'd tell how he and Denise went skinny-dipping late one night in the country club swimming pool and he got caught. Denise ran, leaving her clothes, but he wouldn't tell on her so they locked him up they said to teach him a lesson.

Kim would want to know more about Denise. He'd tell her that in high school—right up that street, see it? Okmulgee High, Home of the Bulldogs—she was known as Denise the piece.

But now he was thinking it wouldn't be fair to say that. It was the reputation Denise had, but you couldn't prove it by him. They had fooled around some but never gone all the way.

Okay, there was Boy Howdy, the variety store where he got his sweatsocks and T-shirts. Ralph's barbershop, he'd stop in once a month for his crewcut. Marino's Bar . . .

It was where he last saw Denise, home that time for Carl's funeral in '86. She was about to marry a country entertainer Ben had never heard of, Wayne Hostetter and the Wranglers, but kept touching him as they had a few beers and talked about things they did twenty years ago, like yesterday.

His close friend in school, Preston Raincrow, mentioned her only once, Preston on the tribal police now, a Muskogee Nation Lighthorseman. They had played basketball together and would write each other when they felt like it. Ben never asked about Denise, but Preston happened to say in a letter she had left Wayne, the country singer, and Ben would think of her—sometimes even while he was living with Kim—and wonder what she was doing. He didn't know why he kept thinking of her.

He drove past her parents' home on Seminole Avenue, but didn't stop. Denise's dad was a lawyer. He liked to bird-hunt and Carl used to take him out to their property on the Deep Fork River.

The Orpheum was showing *Harry Potter* and *Monsters Inc.* That Sunday they went to Point Dume they were going to see *Ocean's Eleven* after Kim talked him out of *Harry Potter.* And if she were sitting next to him right now . . . they might or might not see *Harry Potter,* Kim calling it another kid flick.

II.

Ben took 56 out of town, west, up and around Okmulgee Lake to the bottomland of the Deep Fork, the river that ran through his property to water the groves and keep out the pecan weevils. They still had to spray all summer for fungus and casebearer larva. You had to have the right kind of weather for pecans. Carl used to pray for a spring flood. It got too dry the trees'd start throwing off pecans before they were ready to harvest.

Lydell, his caretaker-foreman, had worked here all his life, first for Carl, and now looked after the property for Ben, who'd transfer money to the bank in Okmulgee and Lydell would draw from it with power of attorney to run the pecan business, pay taxes, hire the spraying done and the work crews, keep production records, make deals with brokers to sell the harvest to a sheller in Texas. Lydell, now in his seventies, would send handwritten reports to Ben. "That tornada come thru and took out 4000 trees. It don't look like we will make our nut this year." Was he being funny? It was hard to tell. If they sorted and bagged a thousand pounds an acre, they'd load eight to ten semis and make money. With last year's freeze they loaded three trucks. The tornado was the year before.

Now, if there hadn't been too much rain Lydell would have already mowed the orchards with a brush hog and raked up the sticks. Ben hoped to see a crew using the shaker today on the trees: mechanical arms gripping the trunk, giving each tree a good shake for half a minute or so, then bringing in the Nut Hustler to gather the pecans from the ground.

Ben turned onto the road that edged along his property and pretty soon there they were off to the left: fifty- and sixty-foot trees on the average looking bare this time of year, a tangle of limbs reaching up to stand dark against the sky, some of the trees growing here seventy years or more.

But no crews in there working, none he could see, only a park of black trees, spiderwebs of limbs and branches, clusters of pecans, untouched. Either the crew started on the other side of the river . . . Wait a minute. Ben raised his foot from the gas pedal to let the SUV coast and slow down. He saw shapes, movement, deep in the trees.

Cattle. A dozen or so cross-Brahmas grazing on papershell pecans.

But there were no cows on the property. Not a one since Carl died.

His great-granddad's original house stood on this road, where Virgil lived till he made his oil money and built a new one in the 1920s, a big California bungalow that was back in the property, the house where Lydell was now living.

Except Lydell was sitting on the porch of the original house, now weathered gray, its porch roof sagging to one side. Ben turned in past a sign that said NO TRESPASSING, one he'd never seen before, and stopped in the yard next to Lydell's pickup, Lydell watching him, the old man's expression taking time to change and now he seemed to be smiling as Ben approached.

"Well, Carl, I'll be God damn. When'd you get in?"

Ben stepped up on the porch.

"Tell me you're being funny."

The old man looked puzzled now. How long had it been since they'd spoken on the phone? Jesus, last Christmas, almost a year. "Lydell, how come you're not up at the other house?"

"What for? This is where I live."

"You used to," Ben said. "Carl died, I said go on live in the new house." The new house as old as some of the oldest pecan trees. Lydell looked puzzled again. Ben said, "Lydell, I'm Ben." And saw the old man's face begin to change again, light coming into his eyes, and Ben heard himself say oh shit.

"Yeah, hell, you're Ben. But you sure look like your daddy."

Ben let that one go. "How're you feeling?"

"Well . . . I don't know. I seen the doctor. He said I'm as good as can be expected."

"Why'd you go see him?"

"I get dizzy at times and have to sit down. I think from the chemicals, that spraying every year as long as I can remember.

I know a boy that did the spraying had to have all his blood drained out and new blood pumped in and he was fine. Went up to Tulsa to work as a gardener."

"But why're you living in this house again?"

"They's only one of me and they's three of them. Four when they have a woman there with 'em. They said they oughta have the house and wrote it into the deal, the lease."

"Lydell, these people leased my house?"

"They leased the property. I musta told you of it in my report. Carl, you can't hire the labor you used to. These fellas come along, offer to work shares on the pe-cans and their cattle both."

"Their cows are in the orchard."

"Again? Goddamn it, I keep telling 'em about that."

"And nobody's working." Ben stepped off the porch to the ruts in the drive to look toward a closed-up barn, a shaker power—hooked to a tractor with a covered cab and a Nut Hustler sitting outside in the weeds and brush. The house where Lydell should be living was a quarter of a mile up this farm road that cut through a grove of pecan trees, the house not in sight from here.

"Lydell, they haven't touched the equipment."

"I'll get on 'em, Carl, don't worry. The one they call Brother? He'll go into town and bring me back my supper if I ask him nice. Get it from the Sirloin Stockade or a TV dinner from Git 'n' Go."

"Lydell, they walk up and say they want to lease the place?"

"Their name's Grooms. A daddy name of Avery and the two boys. Hazen about your age and the younger one they call

Brother. Carl, it's so God damn hard to get labor—Hazen says they'll work the pe-cans, I won't have to lift a hand."

"And they stick you in this shack."

"Hell, it was my home for years and years."

"How'd they come to pick this place?"

"We's related, what they tell me, on my mama's side. They stop by and we's talking, I believe they come from Texarkana."

"Lydell, you have a copy of the lease?"

The old man touched his shirt pocket. "Yeah, it's somewheres. I have to remember now where I put it."

"How long they been here?"

"They come by the first time," Lydell said, "I believe was toward the end of spring, with a real estate woman. Then they come back again and moved in."

"They've been here most of the year," Ben said, "and you never told me?"

"I thought I did, Carl."

Ben drove toward the house, a quarter mile up the farm road, creeping the SUV through the orchard to look at the trees. None of the grounds had been brush-hogged. He angled off the road to get closer to the trees. None had been picked, some with fungus growing on the limbs.

Now the house was straight ahead past cleared land: the house, the structure back of it where pecans were sorted and bagged, an old red barn, a tractor with a rake attached standing outside. The road continued on to a gate that closed off pasture, where a few cows that weren't supposed to be here were grazing. A pickup truck and a Cadillac with a good ten years on it stood at the side of the house, stucco with green trim that needed paint.

Carl had called it a California bungalow design, the kind that didn't look too big till you got up close: the porch in shade, sun shining on bare windows coming out of the steep pitch of the roof. Ben stopped behind the Cadillac and pressed down on the horn to give it a blast. He waited.

Now the screen door swung open and a man in his sixties wearing new bib overalls came out on the porch, his dark hair slicked back, a bottle of beer in his hand. Ben was out of the SUV now walking toward the house. The screen swung open again and a forty-year-old version of the first one appeared. Ben took this one to be Hazen, with the same slicked-back dark hair as his dad but more of it. He wore a striped shirt hanging open with his jeans and what looked like lizard boots. Ben thought Avery, the dad, could stand in for Harry Dean Stanton, looking enough like him to be his twin. Hazen looked like half the stuntmen working today, the kind Kim referred to as rough-trade good-looking, blue-collar guys with an easy slouch to their pose. Trees going to hell and they sat in the house drinking beer.

Ben came to the porch steps and looked up at these Grooms from Arkansas. He said, "I like to know what you're doing in my house."

The one, Hazen, raised his eyebrows saying, "Well, you must be the movie star," sounding glad to see Ben, till he said, "Come to check on us, huh?"

"I'm here to kick you out. This is my home."

Avery said, " 'Fore you start eating anybody's ass out, I'll show you the paper says this property's ourn for two years, stamped and signed by a noterary in the real estate business. You go on get outta here."

Ben said, "You took advantage of an old man didn't know what he was doing." And looked at Hazen. "You tell him you're gonna work shares, only I don't see nothing a-tall getting done. You got cows grazing on pecans falling off trees haven't even been sprayed."

"I changed my mind about growing pe-cans," Avery said. "Gonna test for oil instead. They was some pretty fair wells here at one time and they's always some left."

"The wells were plugged," Ben said. "Cement poured down 'em."

"They's still oil. You heard of stripper wells?"

Ben said, "Look," keeping his tone flat, and it was hard, "even if there's oil, and even if your lease stood up in court, you'd only have surface rights. Mineral rights are something else."

"You mean to tell me," Avery said, "we hit a gusher you don't want to go shares on it? Boy, you're ignorant you think you can make more growing pe-cans. You know what oil's selling for these days?"

No, and he didn't imagine they did either. It wasn't about oil. They were having fun with him, but in a serious way, see where it would lead.

Ben said, "You people are the Grooms, come here from Arkansas?"

Avery, looking past Ben, said, "That's right, and so's this one coming," sounding happy to see whoever it was.

Ben half turned. A pickup came across the open ground to pull up behind his SUV, the driver in a cowboy hat looking this way, then inched up to get his front bumper within a foot of the SUV's rear end. This would have to be the one called Brother, walking toward them now. He had size but looked slow, about twenty-five, a big kid in a cowboy hat and curl-toed boots. The belt cinched around his jeans bore a rodeo winner's buckle, one he must've bought if he didn't steal it. Looking at Ben he said, "Who's this?"

"The movie star," Hazen said.

"No shit."

"You tell by his shades," Hazen said, "and his beauty parlor hair."

"What's he play in movies," Brother said, "queers?"

"Ask him," Hazen said.

Now their big boy was here they were getting to it. Ben told himself to walk away, and said to Avery, "Why don't we have this heard in court?" But couldn't leave it at that. He said to Brother, "You take a swing at me I'll put you on the ground, hard."

Brother stared and Avery said, "Now you got my boy look-ing sideways at you, like he might want to give you an ass-whuppin'."

Ben walked toward Brother saying, "I'm tired, been driv-ing all day. Why don't you whip my ass tomorrow?" Put his hand on Brother's shoulder as he passed and kept walking to the SUV. Ben got in and laid his arm on the windowsill. He said to Brother, "You want to back your truck up a few feet?"

Brother folded his arms and gave Ben a stare that worked

pretty well under the hat brim pointing this way. Brother said, "You can't get out, then you have to stay, huh? Get you ass-whuppin' right now."

Ben turned the key, went ahead a foot or so, revved, said fuck it, and slammed his rear end into the pickup, went ahead, reversed and revved and hit the truck again. Ben slipped out of the space, put the gas pedal on the floor and went into a power slide to head for the road through the trees. He looked back to see Brother going to his truck.

Coming up on the old house Ben stopped at the side of Lydell's porch, the old man still sitting there.

"Lydell, don't you have a daughter lives in Chouteau?"

He said, "Lemme think, I believe Isabel's the one there."

"Go stay with her a while."

Ben turned onto the country road and held his speed at thirty miles an hour with an eye on the rearview mirror. In less than half a minute he saw Brother's truck coming up on him fast, closing in at sixty or better. Ben waited till the truck's hood and windshield filled his rearview, saw the cowboy hat, Brother by himself in there, the big boy wanting to handle this deal on his own. Ben mashed the gas pedal and watched the truck lose ground like it was being sucked away from him. He shot past the road to town doing ninety and held it there, horses in a field raising their heads at the tail of dust rising, the truck behind him hidden as Ben got ready to bring the game to Brother, see if he was any good. Approaching the next intersection he watched the speedometer ease down to forty-five, came to the crossroads and punched his left boot down on the parking brake—tires screaming as the rear wheels locked—cranked the steering wheel a quarter turn, released the brake and let his rear end swing around in a tight one-eighty to head back toward Brother. The fat kid would see from under his cowboy hat a black shape coming dead at him out of the dust and realize, the distance between them closing at top speed, he had seconds to decide how much nerve he had.

Not enough. Brother bailed, swerved off the road to his right, and Ben watched the truck in his mirror dive into the ditch and wedge itself against the bank. Ben stopped and backed up all the way to the truck. Brother, his hat gone, blood coming down his face, turned and looked this way at Ben watching him. Ben shook his head at the dumb kid, put the SUV in gear and headed back to his property.

Avery was still on the porch, sitting in a squeaky wicker chair with green cushions, waiting for Brother to come back with his story, Avery expecting it to be a good one. Hazen was in the house. Avery raised his voice to say, "I told Brother bring him on back here. I was thinking, put that pe-can shaker on him, get his nuts to fall."

Hazen came out to the porch pushing the screen ahead of him.

"I said to Brother, bring him on back, we'll put the pe-can shaker on him."

"I heard you. Where's the number for the real estate office at?"

"By the phone in the kitchen, last I seen of it. You know

Brother'll likely have to chase that *Mercedes* all the way to town to catch it."

Hazen said, "She's pretty, huh? Once we tend to the movie star I might keep her."

"Suppose to be in pitchers—I never heard of him."

"Me neither, but it's what they say."

Both of them heard the car coming and looked out at the yard. Avery said, "Don't tell me," seeing it was the black Mercedes back again but no sign of Brother. Now it circled, bringing the driver's side close to the porch steps. The smoke-glass window lowered and there was Ben Webster looking up at them.

He said, "You all want to settle out of court it's fine with me. My offer, you have till noon the day after tomorrow to get out of my house and off my property. You don't, I'll be back here to run you off."

The smoke window started to go up and Avery said, "Hold it there. Where's Brother at?"

"He needs to get winched out of a ditch," Ben said, "and some Band-Aids."

Avery watched the window slide up all the way and the sporty black SUV circle out of the yard and into the trees, gone. It got Avery frowning, saying to Hazen, "The hell's he talkin about, Brother's in a ditch?"

"Like he put him there," Hazen said.

"Brother was chasing *him.*"

"Brother ain't the issue," Hazen said. "You heard him, he's gonna raise the law on us we don't leave, have troopers out here looking around. You want to stay or not?"

"We ain't gonna move nothing in no two days. Course I want to stay."

"All right, then what do you want done with the movie star?"

"What do you think? Take him off somewheres and shoot him. Hell, Brother'd kill you to do it. Yeah, jes take him off somewheres."

"I saw it coming," Hazen said, "but wanted to make sure." He went inside, walked through the musty smell of the living room to the kitchen, picked up the business card from the counter and dialed the number on it.

Within moments a voice came on saying, "OK Realty, this is Denise. How may I help you?"

Hazen said, "You know who this is?"

There was a pause before she said, "I have a pretty good idea."

Hazen said, "Guess who jes come by here?"

Ben coasted toward Brother standing at the side of the road by his truck and stopped close to him.

"Man, you're a mess."

Bloody from his face to his T-shirt. Brother said, "I busted my goddamn nose," and touched it, barely.

"I see that. Listen, I told your daddy. He ought to be along pretty soon." Ben raised the window, nothing more to say, and continued on toward town.

Doing the one-eighty brought him to life again and got him thinking of Carl, what Carl would say to him: "There you

go, you don't take abuse from those people. You can tell looking at 'em they're dirty. What you said's fine. Get off my
property or I'll fuckin run you off."

They looked serious enough to come after him, and he
couldn't help thinking this situation could be in a movie. The
only thing different, he'd be the good guy for a change. And
it was real life.

III.

Preston Raincrow could trace his people back
more than a hundred and sixty years: some of them from a
Cherokee clan, the Keetoowah, and some from slaves owned
by the Creeks, black slaves brought all the way here from
Georgia or Alabama during the Trail of Tears. His great-
grandma, Narcissa Raincrow, lost a child when she was sixteen—not having any business being with child—and Virgil
Webster hired her as a wet nurse when Graciaplena died giving birth to Carl. Narcissa stayed on as Virgil's housekeeper,
"becoming as close as a man and woman can be," Preston
would say, "till she died a few years ahead of old Mr.
Webster."

Preston and Ben played basketball three years for the Bulldogs, Ben looping the ball toward the basket, Preston finally
growing tall enough to go up for the ball and stuff it. After
high school Preston went to work for Ben's granddad Carl in
the orchards and rode bulls every year in the Okmulgee Invi-
tational, the all-black rodeo they held out at the Creek Nation
arena, fourteen thousand in prize money. Ben told him he was

too lanky for bulls and Preston switched to saddle broncs. It was fun, but didn't offer a living. After a few years he gave up working for Carl and joined the tribal police, became a Muskogee Nation Lighthorseman and drove around in a white Taurus with a gold star on the door.

Ben called the Lighthorseman headquarters from the motel and was told Preston was no longer with them, now working for Russell Exterminating, killing bugs. Ben said, "You're kidding—Preston?" but didn't get a reason or any more information. He called the exterminators to learn Preston was out on his route. Ben left his name and the Shawnee Inn phone number.

Five-thirty, Preston Raincrow hadn't called. Ben was about to try him at home, say hi to Ophelia and find out where he might be. That was when Preston knocked on the door and came in the room in his dark-green exterminator uniform.

The first word he said was "Tenkiller. Man, it does me good to see you," and wrapped his long arms around Ben.

"How'd you find that out?"

"What, calling yourself Tenkiller?" Now he stepped back to look Ben over. "I'd catch a glimpse of you in a movie falling off something, or getting beat up by the good guy, but I wouldn't see your name there at the end? I don't know why I never wrote and asked. So one time I kept stopping the tape to look good. I see 'Ben Tenkiller' there with the stuntmen and I know it's you."

"I used it," Ben said, "to get the job on *Dances with Wolves*, told 'em I was Indian. But then once I was known in the business as Tenkiller I was stuck with it."

"You name yourself after the lake?"

"After the Cherokee with ten notches on his bow the lake was named after. What're you doing killing bugs?"

"You mean 'stead of arresting drunk Indians? I stopped a white guy come driving away from the Elks, weaving all over the road, and I stood at attention while I caught hell for it. What Caucasians do is not the business of a Lighthorseman. The guy even sideswiped a car, said somebody cut him off, two A.M., not a soul on the street. I said fuck it. I said what am I doing working for the law? My great-grandma Narcissa? Her daddy, Johnson Raincrow, was bad as they come and got shot for it in the olden days. Shot while he's sleeping outside on the ground, the only way to take him."

"You gonna turn outlaw?"

"I was thinking you could get me work in the movies. Sonny Samson from here made it big. *One Flew over the Cuckoo's*? The man didn't even talk and was one of the stars."

"You want a beer?"

"I don't need any for a change, but yeah, gimme a cold one." Preston looked around the room of dark wood, the king-size bed, walked over to the balcony and looked out from the second floor. "Man, you could almost dive from here in the swimming pool. But don't try it, you hit your head on the concrete. It's too cold anyway, do any swimming."

Ben got a couple of Buds from the cooler asking Preston how his family was doing. Preston said Ophelia took the kids to her mama's when he quit the cops and stayed drunk for a while. He said, "It ain't hard to act stupid if you put your mind to it. But two weeks of missing them was all I could take." He asked how Ben was doing and Ben told how Kim was killed, falling off a ladder while he's slicing mushrooms, and Preston said, "Did it turn you stupid, get you thinking you're to blame?" Ben said he was handling it. He didn't mention the feeling of expectation, ready for something new in his life. Or ask about Denise, if Preston had seen her lately.

He told about going out to the house and finding these people living there, the Grooms, Avery, Hazen and Brother, and what they'd pulled on Lydell, getting him to lease the property.

"Bring Lydell to court with you," Preston said. "The judge'll let you tear the lease up."

They were seated at the table now, drinking their beer and smoking cigarettes. "They're bad guys," Ben said, "but I can't figure out what they're up to."

"What made you suspect it, big ugly prison tats on their arms?"

"They're not working the place," Ben said. "Letting it go to hell. The barns are closed up, the equipment's all outside in the weather. They got cows in there eating the papershells off the ground."

"That's only criminal in the eyes of a pecan grower," Preston said. "What else you see?"

"Nothing."

"What you suppose are in the barns all closed up?"

Ben said, "If I could get deputies to go out there to take a look—"

Preston was shaking his head. "They have to know what they're looking for."

"But they could go out with subpoenas, couldn't they? Get these guys to appear in court?"

"Once you file a complaint."

"But when's the court date, next year? I want 'em out of there now, so I can still hire the pecans picked. I gave 'em till noon the day after tomorrow."

Preston, starting to grin, said, "Or what?"

"I'd run 'em off."

"You told 'em that, uh? Man, you sound like old Carl. That's what he'd do. Come back from Hollywood and find squatters on his land? He'd go out there with a shotgun and run 'em."

"If he didn't shoot 'em," Ben said.

Preston got up from the table and went to the phone on the desk. "Avery Grooms and Hazen. What's Brother's name?"

"Haven't any idea. But that notebook right there has his license number in it."

Preston dialed, waited a moment and said, "Eddie? Guess who I'm sitting here with having a beer. Our old point guard, man, Ben Webster." He nodded, quiet for a few moments, and said, "I'll tell him that. Listen, what I need, somebody to run two guys name of Grooms, Avery and Hazen, on NCIC." He opened the notebook. "And a license number I'll give you, from Arkansas." Preston spelled the names, gave the number, spoke and listened for a while and said, "Yeah, if you can do it now, I'll buy you three beers." He said to Ben, "Remember

Eddie Chocote, the only freshman made the team our last year? That was Eddie."

Ben said, "Went on to play for Tulsa."

"That's right, and he said you were the quickest guard he ever went down the floor with, and that's counting college ball. But you rather ride bulls."

"It paid," Ben said, "else I'd have to've sold the farm."

"Why keep it? Other than you grew up there."

Ben said, "I have to think about it."

Eddie Chocote came on again and Preston talked to him for a few minutes taking notes, then came over to sit at the table saying, "Hazen have dog bite scars on his left arm?"

"He didn't show me any."

Preston looked at his sheet of notes.

"Hazen Richard Grooms, May 12th, 1967. Served a hundred and thirty-two months in the Cummins Unit over there, Arkansas Department of Corrections. You want to guess what for?"

"Tell me."

"Theft of property and aggravated robbery. Hazen hijacked a highway hauler and they caught him with the tractor. That was, let's see, twelve years ago."

"What about the old man?"

"Avery Louis Grooms, wears dentures, has 'Lucky Dog' tattooed on his left arm. D.o.b. August 5th, 1940. He went down for theft by receiving and was given ninety months in their North Central Unit, the same time Hazen was in Cummins. There's a detainer on him for parole violation. All you do is tell the sheriff and Avery's gone."

Ben said, "I don't know if that would settle it."

"Maybe not," Preston said, "but it would spray their hive, get 'em active." He looked at his notes again. "Next piece of business, the Ford pickup's registered to Jarrett Lloyd Grooms, so Eddie ran him on the crime computer. Date of birth April 10th, 1975. He's six-four and weighs two-forty. That sound like Brother?"

"Those're his dimensions. What'd he do?"

"Went down for third-degree battery on a list of assault indictments, but all he got was a year in the Lonoke County jail." Preston Raincrow laid his notes on the table. He said, "Ben, these people are into hijacking trucks."

"We know Hazen tried it," Ben said.

"I see it as their criminal enterprise. I bet they keep those barns closed tight and locked."

"I never got close enough to tell," Ben said.

Preston took his time. He said, "Maybe I could look into it. Go out there, tell 'em I'm checking on Lyme disease for the county."

Ben said, "Or mad cow."

It got Preston nodding his head. "Yeah, I like mad cow. Say I need to check the feed and the cow shit."

"You think they'll believe you?"

"I wear my exterminator uniform and bring Eddie Chocote along with his sidearm. Tell 'em this mad cow business could be a terrorist plot, like anthrax. Eddie's cool, he'll go along. We find stolen property, we tell the sheriff. We find a meth lab working—speed's big around here—we call the DEA. They'll go out there with marshals. But if we don't get to peek in the barns . . ." Preston shrugged. "You ever in a movie had this kind of situation? Guys you think are bad won't come out of the house?"

"I was one of the guys," Ben said. "I made a run for it and got shot."

"You were good at dying."

"We played guns enough when we were kids. Get shot and go, 'Unhhh, I'm hit,' and fall in the river." Ben thought of what he'd say next, hesitated and then said it. "I almost got shot for real one time, taking a midnight dip in the country club pool."

"And they put you in jail—I remember that. You were with some girl we went to school with."

"Denise Patterson," Ben said.

"That's right, she's Denise Allen now, married twice. The first time to some country singer came through with a show and Denise ran after him. The second time to a guy in Tulsa with oil money left over from the '80s. They got divorced and she come back home. Her folks moved to Hawai-ya and let her have the big house on Seminole Avenue she grew up in. That's where she's at now. Yeah, Denise Allen, in the real estate business, sells farms, sells lake property—"

"How do you know all that?"

"Ophelia does her cleaning. She says Ms. Allen isn't like any other ladies she works for."

"I believe it," Ben said. "One time she wanted me to take pictures of her bare naked, she's sixteen years old, and send 'em to *Playboy*."

"You keep any?"

"I never took the pictures. I was hardshell Baptist at that time," Ben said, "account of Carl had found Jesus. I was reading scripture so I wouldn't go to Hell. I'd go skinny-dipping with Denise and leave my underwear on."

"I remember in school," Preston said, "some guys called her Denise the piece. They said she'd let you screw her long as you were Caucasian. You still Baptist?"

Ben said, "More Unitarian if anything," thinking of Kim. Thinking of her for the first time in hours.

Preston said, "Yeah, Ophelia told her me and you write to each other and she's always asking what you're doing."

"Denise?"

"Who we talking about? I was you, man, I'd give her a call."

IV.

The way Denise met Hazen Grooms: one night in that dark, smoky bar at the Best Western, months ago, he asked her to have a drink with him. He was scruffy, but there was something about his pose she liked, his cool, sleepy eyes, and shrugged, why not, and said she'd have a Margarita. He told her he was a cattleman. Denise said, "You mean you shovel cow shit?" Hazen said he speculated on cattle, oil and land development—looking like he might have five bucks in his jeans. He asked her with his sleepy Jack Nicholson look, "What's a hot number like you doing in Okmulgee?" Denise kept a straight face and laid her OK Realty card on the bar. If this cowboy was into land development he could put up or shut up. Hazen said, "Hmmm," studying the card. He said he had run into a relative of his operated a pecan farm and was talking to him about working shares. He asked Denise if she could put together a lease agreement. When he told her it was the Webster property out in the Deep Fork bottom Denise almost came off her bar stool.

Oh, really?

Since high school she had not stopped thinking of Ben Webster. Not every day, but a lot; in fact more than ever while she was married to those two jerks. She was sure this lease deal would put her in touch with him again. They'd talk about it on the phone and she'd say, "By the way, I'm coming out to the Coast soon." Ben could even come here to look over his tenants and she'd act grown-up for a change, try to be more subtle than she was dreaming up ways to seduce him. Like the skinny-dipping. Like asking him to take nude pictures of her. Like doing a Sharon Stone, sitting with her knees apart in a miniskirt. Nothing worked. Finally she put the question to him in a soft voice, "Ben, are you gay? It's okay if you are." It wasn't, but that's what she said. He looked surprised and told her no, of course not. She said, "Then why don't you want to do it?" He said, " 'Cause it's a sin." It was that fucking Carl's born-again influence. She wondered if it was still a sin now that he lived in Hollywood and was in movies, an Indian, in *Dances with Wolves,* but which one? She caught glimpses of him in other pictures, once she learned which ones he was in. He looked great, even getting shot.

She was dying to see him. He'd called and was coming to the house and she wasn't sure what to wear, if she should go smart or hot.

First Hazen calling with "Guess who just came by."

No, "Guess who jes come by here," and knew right away who he meant—without knowing why she knew it—and felt a twitch in her stomach, or even lower. Hazen said he was calling because now he wanted to buy the property and needed his offering drawn up before the movie star went back to Hollywood, California. He always called Ben the movie star, getting it from Lydell, who hadn't seen a movie since *Gone with the Wind* and assumed any picture Ben said he was in he must've been the star.

"Since you and him are old school buddies," Hazen said, "I bet he'd want you to be in on it and get a nice commission, huh?"

It sounded fishy. Where would he get the money for the down payment, sell his repainted Cadillac?

Hazen said, "I'll find out where he's staying and let you know. See, then you can invite him over, say you got an offer for his property you want to talk to him about." Hazen said, "I can come by your house tonight with the figures. You gonna be home?"

"Tomorrow at the office," Denise said, and wouldn't let him talk her out of it.

She had never allowed him in the house. Several times they had drinks and dinner together because she had nothing to do and was curious about him and would listen to Hazen tell how he'd once rustled cattle with a semi-trailer and had done some prison time in his wild youth, but never associated with the perverts or hogs inside and had kept himself clean, Hazen eating his dinner with his cowboy hat on. Hazen wanted her to know he'd had an outlaw streak in him but now was a straight-shooter looking for the girl of his dreams. If she ever told anybody she'd add, "You have to hear him say it."

Finally, the last time they went out together and he took her home, he started putting the moves on her in his car, the backseat full of engine parts and trash, Hazen kissing and feeling, the straight-shooter smelling of cigarettes, tequila and Aqua Velva, breathing hard through his nose till Denise shut him down with a quiet tone of voice.

She said, "Hazen, please don't," and thought of telling him she was a lesbian, but couldn't bring herself to say the word. So she said, "I'm not used to a man like you. Twice I was talked into getting married, not giving myself time to realize what I was doing, and both times I made an awful mistake. You'll just have to be patient with me."

She didn't have to tell him to get his hand off her tit. He grumbled something and withdrew it. So she didn't have to pull the SIG Sauer .380 she kept in her handbag and shove it under his nose.

It was time to dress for Ben.

The way it turned out it didn't matter what she was wearing.

Denise opened the door. Ben came in. They looked at each other, neither one saying a word. They went into each other's arms for a hug after all these years, kissing each other on the cheek, on the mouth, on the mouth hard, and ended up on the oriental that covered the living-room floor, scrambling to get enough of their clothes off, Ben's windbreaker, his boots—goddamn it, a pair of the newer ones, hard to pull off—his jeans, Denise her cotton sweater, no bra but the panties beneath the skirt, and love was made in a fever that lasted only a few minutes after twenty years of it never having happened.

On the floor side by side looking at each other, both at peace, smiling a little, she said, "Well . . . how've you been?"

He said, "You look better than ever."

She said, "I like your hair like that."

He said, "You're not married, are you?"

"Would it matter?"

"Not now."

She touched his hair. "Where's your cowboy hat?"

"I'm not a cowboy anymore."

"I still have a picture of you I cut out of the paper, riding a bull."

He said, "You want to know something?"

"What?"

He hesitated, but had to say it because it was the reason he was here.

"I think about you all the time."

She said, "Aw, Ben," in a soft way, touching his face, kissing him. Soon they were kissing each other without making a sound as they settled in.

They got cans of beer from the kitchen and took them into the library where they used to kiss and fool around sometimes, but without ever getting too close to doing it. She said, "I guess it's not a sin anymore."

"You remember that?"

"I'd say, 'Why don't we see what it's like.' "

"You already knew."

"Yeah, but not with you and I had to find out. But I wasn't jumping in the sack with everybody. You know how many guys I did it with? Two." She paused. "Actually three while we were in school and I'm Denise the piece? You must've wanted to."

"Sure I did."

She said, "I was absolutely insane over you," and stopped for a moment, looking at him next to her on the cracked leather sofa, her dark hair and part of her face in lamplight. "You're not married, are you?"

He said, "Almost, once," and saw Kim on the beach at Point Dume, what seemed now years ago.

"Why didn't you?"

"I thought I wanted to—"

"But you weren't sure. I wasn't sure, either," Denise said, "when I married Wayne Hostetter, the second-biggest mistake of my life, but it was a chance to get out of town."

Saving Ben from having to talk about Kim, what happened to her, and what he felt now about ever getting married or even serious with a woman, because they didn't have to be married to have something awful happen to whoever she might be. He wasn't convinced that it would, no, but here it was on his mind while Denise was telling him about the country artist, Wayne Hostetter and the Wranglers in their cowboy hats. "I called them Wayne and his Wanglers. He's the only guy I ever heard of puts lifts in his cowboy boots."

"He was your second-biggest mistake," Ben said. "What was your first?"

She said marrying Arthur Allen, an investment banker, the most boring man she'd ever met. "He played golf every afternoon and talked about it all night. It's what golfers do."

"Why didn't you play?"

"It's boring. I saw every movie you were in."

"*Space Sluts in the Slammer Two?*"

"I missed that one."

"I was killed by a space slut. How'd you know about the movies?"

"My cleaning lady."

"Right, Ophelia. Preston told me." He said, "You were interested, huh?"

Denise stared at him. She said, "You big lug, don't you know it's been you all the time? What's that from?"

"A lot of old movies, not any I was in."

She kept staring, not just looking, studying him. She said, "You're a stuntman. That's pretty cool. Do you want to act?"

"I don't think so."

"Stay here and grow nuts? Grow, not go, but you can do both."

"I want to get the place in shape, hire a family to work it and take care of Lydell. I'm thinking of the Raincrows, make Preston the working partner. I thought of that driving over here."

There was a silence and Denise said, "I have a confession to make."

Ben had told her, while they put their clothes back on and went out to the kitchen, the situation with the Grooms.

Forty-eight hours to get out, and he didn't think they'd budge.

"I know those people," Denise said. "I wrote the lease."

"That's your confession? If you hadn't," Ben said, "I doubt we'd be sitting here. Look at it that way."

"But now Hazen says he wants to buy your place, and he's using me to get you two together. You know he's a criminal, or was?"

"I think still," Ben said, "the whole family. Preston looked them up."

"Hazen wants to kill you, doesn't he?" her voice quiet as she said it.

"Any one of them," Ben said. "And if they do and you know about it and can put them away for life . . ."

Ben watched her cross her legs as she thought about it and reach over to pick up her can of beer from the coffee table. Now she was looking at him again.

"I've been ready for Hazen since the first time I met him. He comes here with intentions of doing us harm I'll shoot him. My dad gave me a gun a long time ago, and I'm licensed to carry it. But you know what? You better move your car from the drive. Park it in town somewhere."

"It won't be here," Ben said. "I'm meeting Preston later on. He's looking into the Grooms, see if he can find out, as he says, what kind of criminal enterprise they're in. I always like talking to Preston."

"So you can stay a while?"

"I'm not in any hurry."

"Tell me some Hollywood stuff."

"Jack Nicholson always carries an ashtray in his pocket."

"What about—like I heard some stars actually do it in their love scenes?"

"I wouldn't be surprised, but I've never been needed on that kind of set. What else you want to know?"

"Ben, have you really been thinking about me?"

V.

Preston Raincrow got home and threw a football around with his two boys, went in the house and kissed Ophelia and his little girl, smelled what was cooking and poured himself two ounces of Jim Beam. He sipped on the drink thinking of Avery Grooms and his two white trash boys, thinking if Avery was picked up on the detainer and held for Arkansas, it could cause his boys to act stupid and become nasty and they could be picked up, too. Preston had one more drink for the pleasure of it—he didn't need courage—and phoned the young sheriff of Okmulgee County, a reasonable-enough Caucasian boy Preston had played football with this time, and told about the detainer. "Avery Grooms, done most of ninety months, come out and must've blew his parole." He said, "You know the Webster place. That's where he's at." Preston suggested the young sheriff bring some backup along, the man had his two sons with him and they weren't likely to sit still, watch their old dad taken away cuffed. He listened and said, "Anytime. I'm always glad to help you out."

The Raincrows were finishing their supper when the phone rang. Preston listened to the young sheriff say it was on for tonight and he could come if he wanted. Preston sat at the

table again and ate the rest of his rice pudding before calling
Eddie Chocote.

Hazen put aside the early part of the evening
to check motels, see where a Ben Webster was registered,
came to the Shawnee Inn and the desk clerk said, "Yes sir, he
sure is," but wouldn't give up the room number till Hazen
flashed a federal badge and ID he'd bought in Biloxi, Mississippi, and used from time to time and was told, "Room two-
twenty, overlooking the patio and the swimming pool." The
clerk wanted to know if Mr. Webster was in some kind of
trouble and was told, "He sure is, partner."

Hazen returned to his favorite bar, the dark, smoky one at
the Best Western, and drank Margaritas while he thought
about what to do with Denise. If she'd have come across once
or twice he'd feel better about her. As cold sexu'lly as the
woman was he believed he could set her afire and bring her to
her . . . get her to come. Hazen thinking now that if Brother
took care of the movie star that'd be out of the way and he'd
have had nothing to do with it. He could stay around and take
his time with the real estate lady. If it ever came to putting a
pistol on her, like a last resort . . . Hell, he didn't even know
where he'd aim.

His cell phone made its noise. It was Brother trying to
keep his voice low. "They come and put handcuffs on Daddy,
saying he's going back to Arkansas."

The Margaritas worked to Hazen's favor, allowing him to
believe he was cool. He asked Brother, "You say anything stupid to 'em?"

"They want to know who I was, see my driver's license. Asked could they look around. Daddy told 'em they could go fuck theirselves."

Hazen said, "Shit." That kind of talk could bring 'em back with warrants. "They still there?"

"Yeah, they's still here. Jesus Christ, you coming?"

"A bunch of 'em?"

"Three Crown Vics, 'Sheriff' on the doors big. A Taurus with 'Muskogee Nation Lighthorseman' on it. They got their headlight beams on the house, lightnin' it up. The deputies are wearing vests and carrying shotguns, like they expect we's armed. Daddy's saying, 'I never detained nobody. The hell you talking about.'"

"Don't even know he's wanted. Been for five years."

"Hazen, you coming?"

"For what, kiss him goodbye?"

"They's putting him in the car, pushing his head inside. You don't get over here they gonna be gone."

Hazen said, "I got no business with those people. Soon as they leave, come on meet me here at the bar. I found out where Mr. Webster's staying."

It quieted Brother. He said, "Yeah?" interested.

"They come with warrants, we don't want to be anywhere near the place. But I don't want to leave till you take care of Mr. Webster."

"Why you saying me?"

"You're the one has the score to settle. Look at your goddamn nose. Do what Daddy said, shoot him in the head."

"What're you gonna do?"

"Don't fuck up and I won't have to do nothing."

Preston was with Eddie Chocote, the Lighthorseman, the last one out, trailing the taillights of the sheriff's cars but not all the way. Eddie killed his lights and turned from the farm road into the grove of pecan trees, creeping now in the dark, not too far. . . . "Right here," Preston said. Next thing, turn the car around and watch for headlights: going out would be Brother, coming in, most likely Hazen. The plan: if Brother leaves, Eddie follows him to see where he goes. Preston would stay here and look in the barns. Maybe even the house.

Eddie said, "Looking for what?"

"I don't know—whatever I find."

Eddie said, "You have your sidearm?"

Preston, getting out of the car, said, "I don't need it. I gave it to Ben."

Driving back to the Shawnee Inn he didn't think of the Grooms once. It was all Denise, her scent on him, her asking, "Do you really think about me?" And telling her almost every day.

But not saying it was with a longing, or even understanding why her face kept showing up in his mind, until he saw her again. He was in love with her was the reason. Had always been in love with her except . . . Carl was the problem back then, Carl and Jesus, Carl getting him bummed about going to Hell, while Denise's idea was to "experience life" and she dared him to do things with her. Like buying weed in the black section of Okmulgee, Denise asking the young guys

about their life and listening to stories about dope house busts
and guys getting shot, Denise natural, standing there in her
miniskirt, but not putting on any kind of airs, and they were
nice to her. She talked him into leaving college to get his
rodeo ticket, and by that time they weren't even seeing much
of each other.

She had been way ahead of him back then and now he'd
caught up. When they were still on the floor, settling in, and
for a while they were quiet, he said to her, "Denise . . . 'You're
the reason God made Oklahoma.' "

She looked at him and without changing her expression
said, " 'There's a full moon over Tulsa, I hope it's shining
on you.' "

Ben said, " 'In Cherokee County there's a blue norther
passin through.' "

Denise said, "Boy, have I missed you."

"I'm surprised you know that one."

"Wayne covered it with some girl, but their cut didn't
compare to David Frizzell and Shelly West."

"That song'd come on," Ben said, "and if I wasn't thinking
of you already I would then."

In the library, on their second beer, she said, "Now that
you're a grown man, how many girls have you slept with in
your life?"

He began thinking about it, looking for faces.

She said, "You're counting?"

"You asked how many."

"I meant in round numbers."

"About ten."

"In over twenty years?"

"Wait. Fourteen."

"What'd you have, four at one time?"

"In one afternoon, at a whorehouse in San Francisco. With some rodeo buddies."

"I bet that was a party. Four times isn't bad."

"Average for a bull rider."

"How about some who weren't hookers?"

"Yeah, about ten. I spent time with a girl when I first went out to the Coast and . . . a couple years with a girl one other time."

"You were in love."

"To some extent. The one, we talked about getting married 'cause she wanted to have a child—even though in Hollywood you don't have to be married." He wasn't going to ask Denise how many men she'd slept with, but thought of something close to it and said, "You ever cheat on your husbands?"

She took her time, close to each other on the couch, and put her hand on his thigh. She said, "I gave you the wrong idea. Really, the only reason I asked—I've imagined rodeo bunnies and starlets coming at you in packs."

"Packs?"

"Droves. I thought you'd say, modestly, 'Oh, only a few hundred,' and it could be true. I didn't bring it up to compare notes with you. I was never Denise the piece and I don't sleep around. You want to know if I ever cheated on those two jerks? I did once. When I was married to Arthur, bored out of my mind."

"And a little horny."

"Probably. I could've had a shot at the club tennis pro, but I didn't."

"Who was the guy?"

"The UPS man. Arthur goes, 'You're doing what seems to me an inordinate amount of ordering from catalogues lately.' Swear to God. The UPS guy was funny and kinda cute, but it was recreational, no way it would come to anything." She shrugged and looked at her hand on his leg.

Ben said, "You think you'll marry again sometime?"

She looked up at him, her smart eyes holding his, looked away and nodded a couple of times like she was thinking about it and came back to him.

"Let's say I'm madly in love."

"Yeah . . . ?"

"And he's the kind of guy isn't afraid to ride a two-thousand-pound pissed-off animal with horns."

Ben said, "I doubt he'd step up on one today."

Denise said, "It wouldn't matter." She said, "Ben, I'll marry you first thing in the morning if you'll spend the night."

And he said—

He turned off the interstate to pull up in front of the Shawnee Inn.

He didn't know what to say and she told him not to say anything if he didn't want to. She said, "I'm not putting you on the spot, I'm telling you how I feel."

That was when he said, "But it's like we just met," and she started shaking her head, smiling at him.

Ben went up the stairway and along the hall toward his room. He saw the guy at the end of the hall by the Coke machine, a big guy looking this way, about to put money in the machine, but now was coming toward Ben in a hurry—Brother in his cowboy hat—running, pulling a gun, a revolver, from under his jacket. Ben got to 220, shoved the card in the lock slot and a goddamn red light came on, shoved the card in again and now the green light showed and the door opened as Brother reached him. All Ben had time to do was step and jab a left hand hard into the nose with adhesive tape on it, stopping Brother long enough for Ben to get in the room and this time hit Brother in the face with the door as he tried to swing it closed and heard Brother yell out as he stumbled back, Ben already crossing to the balcony, sliding open the glass and now was looking down at the pool about twenty feet from the building, no lights showing, Ben not knowing how deep the water was. He heard the door to the hall bang open and pressed himself against the stonework framing the balcony, felt handholds between the stones, and hoisted himself to the tarred gravel roof, rolling onto it as Brother reached the balcony.

Ben looked around. There was no door to a stairs going down, only metal shapes housing the air-conditioning, no place to hide. He could stay up here if Brother was afraid to climb the stonework. But if Hazen was around—he couldn't be too far.

Ben got down flat on the roof, put his eyes over the edge and there was Brother with his gun raised, pointing straight up at Ben and firing in the night as Ben rolled away from the edge and crawled back a few yards before getting to his feet. He'd have to run and dive for the pool—the way he dove off the roof of a motel when they were filming at Angola, the Louisiana State Prison, did it on a bet and caught hell from the stunt coordinator. "You want to lose your SAG card, asshole?" Hell no, it was worth $636 a day whether he worked a stunt or not. He remembered now the trouble he had at Denise's trying to get his new boots off in a hurry. He'd have to leave them on—goddamn cowboy boots when he ought to be wearing high-top sneakers.

Brother surprised him.

Ben started for the edge—four strides and dive out as far as he could—and Brother's cowboy hat and shoulders appeared above the roof edge, arms clinging tight to the tarred gravel, Brother trying to raise the gun and hold on at the same time. The gun fired in the moment Ben reached Brother to kick him in the face: Brother going back, falling, Ben pressing to keep his balance and then lunging out at the dark, Brother missing the balcony but not the concrete floor of the patio, as Ben landed flat in the water in his wool shirt and his windbreaker and began swimming to the side of the pool, till he found out he could walk.

Denise opened the door. Ben gave her time to look at him wringing wet and say whatever she wanted.

She said, "You change your mind?"

VI.

The first thing Ben did, dripping on the kitchen floor, was call Preston. Ophelia said, "Hey, Ben, love your movies," and they talked a while. Preston wasn't home but she'd have him phone.

Denise helped him take his clothes off and put them in the dryer—shirt, jacket, socks, everything but his boots—poured a couple of vodkas, and they stood in the kitchen, Ben in a terry-cloth robe stretched tight on him, while he told Denise about Brother.

She said, "You sure you're not making it up? It sounds like a movie. I can hear the score, 'You're the Reason God Made Oklahoma.'"

Standing there in the kitchen looking at each other, Ben said, half singing it, "'I work ten hours on a John Deere tractor just thinking of you all day.'"

Denise did the same with "'I've got a calico cat and a two-room flat on a street in West L.A.'" and stopped there. She said, "But the song has it turned around. I'm here and you're the one in L.A." She said, "You're going back, aren't you? Once you get Preston or someone to work your place?"

Ben hesitated. That was the idea and he could say yeah. He could say yeah, why don't you come with me? It was in his mind.

The phone rang before he could say anything.

Preston telling how Avery Grooms had been picked up on the detainer and what he found in the barns. "Ben, was a big Peterbilt tractor in one and all kind of truck parts in there. Big Cummins diesel engine, crankshafts, axles. What they do, Ben, hijack a truck, bring it there and go over it like ants taking apart a magnolia leaf. See, then they sell to wholesalers in that criminal enterprise. The diesel engine they can get six, eight thousand for."

"A lot of work," Ben the eight-second man said, "for what they make off it."

"Yeah, well, these are working-type people, they don't know no better."

Ben told about Brother and Preston said, "I gave you my Smith, whyn't you shoot him?"

"It was in my bag, I didn't have time to get it out."

"If you had, would you've shot him?"

"If I couldn't club him with it. I've done it."

"You mean in a movie." Preston said he'd find out about Brother and call back.

Once Ben's clothes were dry he peeled off the robe and got dressed, Denise watching, looking right at him as he stepped into his shorts and jeans and pulled them up—the way he remembered when they were little kids and she always wanted to see his thing and he'd tell her to close her eyes or turn around. Not now. He felt natural, the way he liked to think of himself with Denise. More natural than with any woman he could think of. Even Kim.

And there she was, bringing along the other women.

He wasn't going to tell Denise about them, but now he wanted to—even knowing pretty much what she'd say.

Preston phoned.

"City police and the sheriff both got the call, shots fired at the Shawnee Inn. They got over there to find Jarrett Lloyd Grooms, laying by the swimming pool unconscious, and took him to Memorial. Brother's busted up cheekbones to toes, messed up his mouth, has knees that bend the wrong way. They wrote him for having the gun and attempting to break and enter."

"They think he's a burglar? What about the shots fired?"

"Gun went off when he fell. They want to close it."

"They have Hazen?"

"No sign of him. He must've took off."

Ben hung up, gave Denise the report, and she said, "You're staying tonight, aren't you?"

"Yeah, but I want to tell you something."

They were in the kitchen now, Denise pouring vodka.

"You know my mother left right after I was born."

"Your dad was dead and that part of her life, along with you, was over."

"She died of drugs and alcohol."

"Yeah . . . ?"

"You remember Carl?"

"Honey, Carl leaves his imprint on you."

"His wife, my grandmother Kitty, walked out on him after a year."

"Girls named Kitty don't think much of becoming grand-mothers."

"Virgil's wife, my great-grandmother, died having Carl."

"I won't comment on that."

"And the girl I was living with, Kim, a stuntwoman, fell off a ladder at home and fractured her skull."

Denise said, "You're kidding."

"No, she did."

"I mean about what you're thinking, that I could be next in line. Tell me you're kidding."

"Carl's the one pointed it out. He said we don't seem to have any luck with women."

Denise said, "Carl?" She said, "*Carl* told you that? Carl told stories, things he did as a marshal? My dad said most of it wasn't true."

"Your dad represented guys Carl arrested."

"He predicted things, crops, the weather—where to find game—my dad told me about that, too. He said Carl was always wrong. You lived half your life with him and you didn't know that?"

"His stories were great," Ben said. "His predictions, I never paid any attention to them. It's just, every once in a while I think about what he said."

Denise shook her head. "Ben, your granddad didn't know shit. Remember that and you'll quit thinking of yourself as a lady killer."

"I thought you might fall on the floor laughing."

"That's too obvious." She finished her drink and looked at Ben in fluorescent kitchen light and said, "You're perfect for me and I've known it since I was a little girl. But you're too glum." She took the drink from his hand and placed it on the counter.

"Let's go to bed so I can wake you up."

Brother never showed. By the time Hazen realized it and quit talking to the waitress he'd had five Margaritas following a few beers earlier. He called the farm and let it ring. What was he supposed to do now, call the police? Y'all holding my little brother? Call the hospital, see if he got hurt fucking up somehow? He probably sassed the troopers and they put him in detention. Next they'd be out to the farm with warrants. Shit, it was time to move on. Tomorrow, after he'd settled accounts.

Hazen went out to the desk and took a room for the night.

Tomorrow he'd go to Denise's house first thing, before she left for the real estate office, and have her call the famous movie star nobody ever heard of and tell him to get his ass over there.

They were still in Denise's double bed under the covers, putting off getting up. She said, "I imagined you'd snore, but you don't."

"You do, a little."

"Really? No one's ever told me."

"I gave you a kick and you stopped."

"I suppose you want breakfast—eggs, the whole thing?"

"I like just a sandwich, if you have any leftovers."

"Leftover what, you think I cook dinner for myself?"

"You know how?"

"Is it important to you?"

He said, "I haven't thought of Hazen once."

She said, "Then why bring him up."

"Later on I have to see a lawyer."

She said, "Let's brush our teeth and go for another, okay?"

"After you." He watched her get out of bed naked and go in the bathroom. He waited for the full frontal shot when she came out, and heard the doorbell. He got out of bed and went over to the bathroom to tell Denise through the door someone was here.

She came out wrapping herself in a pink kimono. "It's the paperboy. He comes to collect once a month." She said, "Don't get dressed. Put the robe on and we'll have a cup of coffee first, okay?"

She picked up her handbag from the vanity and went downstairs barefoot.

She was seriously thinking of selling the house, but would hold on for a while, see what happens. It was way too big for one person, dark, sort of Victorian, frosted-glass panels in the double doors of the entrance. She could see a figure waiting on the porch, a dark shape more than an actual person, opened the door and said to Hazen Grooms, "You're not the paperboy."

"What I am," Hazen said, "is hungover. You get horny when you're like that? Man, I sure do." He stepped inside and took the lapel of her kimono between his fingers, feeling it, saying, "Honey, you're a sight for horny eyes. I bet you got nothing on under there, have you?" He looked past her saying, "What I need more'n anything right now is a cold beer. Get the spiders outta my head." He started across the foyer saying, "I bet they's some in the fridge," and went on through the hall that passed beneath the staircase landing to the big kitchen in the back of the house.

Denise followed, handbag hanging from her shoulder, not saying a word. She opened the refrigerator, brought out a can of Bud and placed it on the table in front of Hazen. He said, "We not talking this morning. Still seepy-eyed? We could go back to bed, you want." He popped open the can and Denise watched him pour the beer down his throat, his Adam's apple bouncing as he swallowed, watched him lower the can, his eyes shining wet, and say, "Jesus, I've come back to life."

She brought a glass ashtray from the sink and placed it

with her handbag on the other end of the table from Hazen. Now she took a pack of Winston and a Bic lighter from the bag, lit a cigarette and dropped the pack and lighter back inside.

"Gotta have that first smoke, huh?" Hazen said. "What I want you to do for me is call Mr. Ben Webster, get him to come over here."

"Why?" Denise said.

"Settle our business."

"I thought you changed your mind—your dad going back to prison and all."

It got him to hesitate. "Where'd you hear that?"

"My cleaning lady."

"Your *cleaning* lady." Hazen squinting at her now. "How'd she know?"

"What difference does it make?" Denise said, and blew smoke at him. "You're leaving, aren't you?"

Now he changed again, using his sly Jack Nicholson eyes. "If I am," Hazen said, "we got one last chance to go upstairs and fall in love."

She saw Ben in the terry-cloth robe too small for him appear in the doorway behind Hazen, and said, "I don't think Tenkiller would like it."

Hazen said, "Who?"

Now Ben came in past Hazen to Denise's end of the table, looking around to say, "I wouldn't waste any time. I think you ought to get out of here's fast as you can."

Hazen put his beer on the table and stared at Ben in the fluffy skin-tight robe, the sleeves short of his wrists. "Jesus Christ," Hazen said, "you go around in women's things, you're actu'lly queer, aren't you? One of those fellas likes to take it in the butt. You hear the one, the Indin goes in the whorehouse with a bushel of corn?"

"Front hole money hole," Denise said, "back hole corn hole. I told it to Ben in the eighth grade."

Ben remembered it and turned his head to Denise. Hazen said, "Look at me, goddamn it," and they saw him holding a black semiautomatic pistol on them but mainly on Ben, a big one Denise believed was a Colt .45, like one her dad used to have, Hazen saying now, "I'm through talking," raised the gun to eye level and put it dead center on Ben.

Ben said, "You're gonna shoot me? For what? It won't get you my land."

Hazen sighted down the barrel. "I'm not talking to you no more."

Denise's hand went into the bag close in front of her.

Ben said, "How's Brother?"

It stopped Hazen because—Denise saw it—he didn't know and had to ask.

"What happen to him?"

Her hand came out of the bag and laid the pack of Winston on the table.

"He fell off a roof," Ben said. "He won't die, but has to be put back together."

"Goddamn it," Hazen said, "what'd you do, push him off?"

Denise's hand went back into the bag.

"I'm trying to get away from him," Ben said, "and he's shooting at me up there, and he lost his balance."

"You care so much," Denise said, "why don't you go to the hospital and see him?" She waited a moment and said, "You shoot Ben you'll have to shoot me, too, won't you?" Threw that in and got Hazen to look at her and saw his eyes lose their fire, his eyes turning heavy so she'd think he was cool.

"You know your brother," Ben said. "He likes to fight but doesn't know how. He's too quick on the trigger."

"He's a moron," Denise said to Hazen. "That's why you never let him hang around with you. I really think you ought to take off while you have the chance."

Ben said, "Why bust your ass dealing in truck parts? If I was a hardcase like yourself, shit, I'd rob banks. My granddad, a famous deputy U.S. marshal in his day, used to tell me robbing banks took nerve, but was the quickest way to get your hands on real money. Even if you get caught and put away, you're looked up to in prison."

Denise said, "Really? Is that true?"

Ben said, "Yeah, bank robbers are among the elite," and looked at Hazen. "You've done time. Isn't that right?"

"Hijackers," Hazen said, "don't take any backseats to nobody."

"It's a lot of work though, huh? Heavy work." Ben said, "You want another beer?"

"No," Denise said, "he's running out of time. Let him go."

Hazen put his sleepy eyes on her, looking more tired than cool, and she softened her tone saying to him, "Go on, Hazen, get out of here while you can." She paused a moment and said, "For my sake. Please."

And it seemed to move him. Hazen said, "Sometimes it works," shaking his head, "and sometimes it don't." He looked at Denise again to say, "This one wasn't my trip," and walked out with his big Colt .45.

Neither one of them moved until they heard the front door slam.

"What did you mean," Ben said, "you told him to leave for your sake?"

Denise's hand came out of the bag holding her SIG Sauer and laid it on the table.

"So I wouldn't have to shoot him."

"You think you would've?"

"If it looked like you and I were through before we even got started? I'm not a victim type." She said, "That man is really stupid, isn't he?"

"Carl said nine out of ten criminals have the brain of a chicken."

"Your old granddad, known for his wisdom."

"He could tell a story," Ben said.

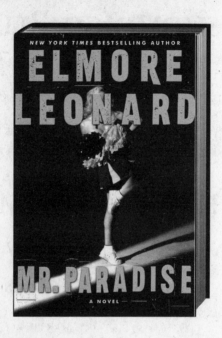

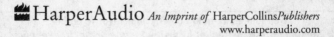